Book II of The Immortal Epic

IMMORTAL CONQUEST

BY
KEVIN D. BLACKMON

ASCENDANT PUBLISHING
NORTH CAROLINA
2011

Also by Kevin D. Blackmon

The Immortal Epic
Immortal Journey

IMMORTAL
CONQUEST

ACT I

2011 AD

CHAPTER I

THE TWINS RETURN

Kieran and Kelena have returned from their tour of the world. They have been gone nearly a year. During that time, I started my own publishing company and released my first book, Immortal Journey: Book I of The Immortal Epic.

I must say, it's been a tough year. By releasing my book, I inadvertently painted a target on myself. A number of my fellow humans, if I can still call them that, have shown distaste for my first novel. They haven't physically attacked me, but they have shaken their religious beliefs at me. I'm not telling people what to believe. I'm simply saying not to believe whole-heartedly what other people say; they could be wrong, too. Do your own research, and decide for yourself. No one can tell you what to believe; only you can. Personally, I think we are too small to fathom just how big it all is.

I was, however, attacked by creatures that were thought to exist only in the minds of madmen. I've had some close calls, to say the least. Thankfully, my family hasn't been hurt, so I assume these creatures still live under Manius' rule of remaining hidden from the eyes of mortal men.

Unfortunately, I've put Seraphine in danger. She had come back to the States to spend the summer with me and meet my family. As expected, my mom absolutely adored her. It is very seldom that I have a girlfriend, so it was a welcomed surprise.

One of Seraphine's favorite movies is Young Frankenstein. Since I had never seen it, we watched it together. I found it to be a delightful movie with a brilliant cast.

I also took her to the coffee shop where I used to work. She loved their hot chai. Of course, I couldn't drink it, but it smelled wonderful.

She told me that she was becoming bored with being just a pretty spokeswoman at tech shows. She's looking for a job in genetic engineering and has already been applying at laboratories in the United States and Europe. She asked if I would move with her to wherever she needs to move. I told her that I was close to my family but couldn't imagine letting her go, so I would move with her.

After spending a wonderful summer together, I was sad to see her head back home to Italy, but she had several shows to attend. She asked if I wanted anything from Europe. I told her, I just wanted her to come back. She said for me not to worry because she would be back, and she kissed me goodbye.

Two days later, she messaged me from her phone saying there were three strangers in her house waiting for her, and they changed into werewolves! One of the beasts told her that their master was offering a reward for bringing me in alive, but they only needed an ear from her! She was barely able to get away from them. She said she had been hurt, but she would be okay. She told me that she couldn't go home, and she couldn't see me for fear of leading her attackers to me.

I pleaded with her to come back, but she felt it best to distance herself from me. I told her that I loved her and that we should face this together, but she can be stubborn at times.

We have been staying in contact by email only, but I haven't heard from her in weeks! I don't even know where she is at the moment. I sure hope she is okay.

As a child, her mother left her with a human couple. Seraphine inherited their Italian villa after their passing and lives there when she's on that side of the Atlantic.

She had been hiding amongst humans her entire life. It's much easier in this day and age to pass off elven ears as a cosmetic procedure, but it would seem Manius still has agents hunting down the old races.

With Kieran back, perhaps he can help me find a solution to this problem so I can see her again, and I can get back to a normal life. Well, as normal as a vampire can expect.

"Whatcha doin'?" Kelena's voice startled me. I turned to see her standing in the doorway holding a wrapped gift. She was wearing white shorts and a blue tank top with matching Chuck Taylors. Her thick, strawberry blonde curls fell over her shoulders. The gift she held was about two feet by one foot, wrapped in white paper with a big, gold bow.

"I was just writing in my journal," I answered, saving my progress and closing the program.

"I brought you a gift," she said cheerfully.

"For me?" I asked, a big smile spreading across my face. I left the computer and walked over to her. "You didn't have to get me anything."

Handing me the present, she said, "I saw this and knew you would like it, so I got it for you."

"Well, thank you so much," I told her, sitting the gift on my bed. I untied the bow and tore the wrapping away to reveal a Marvel limited edition statue. "Silver Surfer! Oh wow! It's awesome! I love it. Thank you." I hugged her tight for the wonderful gift.

"You are very welcome. I'm glad you like it."

As I looked over the box containing a statue of my favorite superhero, Kelena added, "There's also something I want to tell you."

"Yeah?" I questioned, turning my attention to her.

"I'm not sure how to tell you, so I'm just gonna say it," she began. "The choice to make you a vampire wasn't entirely Kieran's."

"Okay."

"At the turn of the twentieth century, my brother chose a young lady to give eternal life. She refused the gift, but it was I who chose you, Kevin."

Confused by what she was telling me, I didn't know what to say.

As if she wasn't ready for her own words, she pulled my desk chair out and sat down. "Centuries ago, when Dirk ripped out my heart, and I lay dying in Kieran's arms, my thoughts, my consciousness, entered into my brother's mind."

Still not knowing what to say, I sat on the bed and listened to her story.

"It may not have been my body," she continued, "but I was occasionally able to work through it. I pushed him to be faster, stronger." She stared off as she remembered the past. "Sometimes I felt I was more attuned to his senses than even he was," she added with a laugh.

Finally speaking, I asked, "Did he know when you had control of him?"

"It wasn't like I took control of him. It was more like I directed his attention or urged him to do better," she explained, wondering if she was even describing it properly. "The thought of me being with him crossed his mind on occasion, but how would you know if your thoughts weren't your own?"

"Uh, I don't know," I answered, shaking my head. "So what happened the day Kieran and I put your heart back into your body?"

"My body was brought back to life, but it transformed immediately into the werewolf, acting only on its primal instincts. My consciousness wasn't yet in my body. I saw it all happening through Kieran's eyes."

"What about when he carried you away from me and submerged you in the pool of blood?"

"Kieran allowed the werewolf to bite him, and I was able to transfer back into my body. The hot plasma that courses through Kieran destroyed me but not before the power of the phoenix was able to take hold."

"Wow," I said, shaking my head. "And how long

were you trapped within Kieran's mind?"

She stared off again, her face blank. "Nearly fifteen centuries," she finally answered as if she herself couldn't believe it.

There was a long moment of silence between us before she broke into laughter. Her laugh made me laugh.

"I hated that bitch Sylvia for leaving my brother . . . but I am grateful for all that she did for us," she added, glad to be alive. She held her hand out to me, so I took it. "I am also grateful for you giving my body life again with your blood."

"You gave me a good scare," I laughed, remembering being cornered by a blood-soaked werewolf. Just thinking about it again caused me to shiver.

"I'm sorry I scared you," she apologized with a laugh. She caressed my face, but then gave me a couple of light slaps before pulling away, snickering. "I found you through him," she said, turning her eyes toward mine. "I know you carry great pain within your heart."

I looked away, thinking about what she could know about me.

"You forget, I don't have to feed on you to see your thoughts and memories," she admitted. "I know your heart leads you, and it's your heart that is often broken. Most humans are cruel and cold, but you, you have the heart of an elf. You try so hard to be a good person, and when your love isn't returned, you feel you're still not good enough."

Blood tears welled up in my eyes, and a drop fell from my lashes to be quickly caught by Kelena. I looked at her through my red stained eyes. She held her hand out for me to see the crimson tear.

"The humans who have hurt you don't know how much heart there is in a single tear, and they will never know because they are too cruel and cold to see."

I couldn't hold it back any longer. Tears began streaming down my face. Kelena sat next to me, and I collapsed into her arms. She said nothing for a long moment while I cried. I finally lifted my head from her shoulder to see that I had stained it with blood. "I'm sorry about your shirt," I apologized with a weak laugh.

"Ah, don't worry about it." She wiped her hand over her shoulder, and the blood seemed to simply evaporate away.

"I have some Immortal Journey tee shirts. I need to give you one anyway." I opened the box that held two dozen brand new shirts and handed her one.

She looked at the front, and then turned it around to look at the back before returning it to me.

"No, you can have it," I told her.

"The clothes that I wear are formed from a thought," she explained. The blue tank top that she was wearing immediately changed to the shirt I offered to give her, a white and red ringer tee with the words, "I AM IMMORTAL" printed on the front, and "IMMORTAL JOURNEY by Kevin D. Blackmon" on the back. "Thank you, but you don't need to be giving away your product; you can't make any money that way," she said, giving me a kiss on the cheek. "Now, email this elf of yours; I'd like to meet her. And for her sake, she better not break your heart," she added with a grin and a slap of her hand.

I laughed and wiped my face. I had blood all over my hands. I stood to go wash up when Kieran appeared behind his sister.

He was shocked to see me. "What happened?" he asked, looking from me to Kelena. "You just got here!" he told her. "What'd you do, hit him? Did she hit you, Kevin?"

"No. She didn't hit me," I answered, walking around them to the bathroom.

I turned the sink on and began washing the blood from my hands while I looked at myself in the mirror. I looked terrible. Both, Kelena and Kieran stood in the bathroom doorway watching me clean up.

"We were just talking," I began to explain, washing my face. "She stirred up some emotions, and well, it's hard to hide your pain when you cry tears of blood." I grabbed the towel off the rack to dry my face but stopped to ask him, "Can't you see my thoughts just as easily as Kel?"

"I can but prefer not to. So what did she say to get you stirred up like this?"

"Oh, come on. I just got cleaned up," I told him, putting the towel back on the rack. I pushed past him and his sister, so I wouldn't feel cornered in the bathroom.

"He's having girl trouble," I heard Kelena whisper to him.

I threw my hands up and stepped outside on the porch. The sun was still high in the sky and shining bright. I stood in the shade of the porch, but the brightness made my eyes squint. My heightened sense of hearing could still hear Kelena explaining the situation.

"Kevin's very particular when looking for a girlfriend, much like you, if you remember. He's only liked a handful of girls in his entire life."

"If you're going to tell me, I might as well look for myself," I heard Kieran say. "I wanted Kevin to tell me."

"Just listen," she ordered. "Each new love in his life must seem better than the last, but none of the girls he's opened up to has shared the same feelings for him." Kelena paused for a moment and sighed heavily before continuing. "He takes the loss of those he loves very hard. He carries a scarred heart. He's been a vampire for a little more than a decade now, and he already feels the pain of immortality."

Listening to her again brought all those familiar feelings of rejection to the surface, and I felt my eyes become damp again.

Kieran passed it off as just part of the transition, saying, "He'll be okay. The first lifetime is the hardest."

"I think you're missing the point," Kelena argued. "He doesn't want to end up like us! He doesn't want to live for millennia, alone in a cave, dreaming of a different life!" She took a moment to calm herself. "He's met an elf. She seems to care about him, but his book has drawn unwanted attention from those who follow Manius' rule. They kill elves, and now, Kevin doesn't know where she is because she hasn't spoken to him in weeks!"

"Where'd he meet an elf?" Kieran asked.

"He met her in D.C.!" I heard her answer with a stamp of her foot. "Haven't you read his book?" she questioned him harshly.

I heard no answer from Kieran.

"Immortal Journey," Kelena told him. "There is a whole box of 'em on his bedroom floor. Read it."

She walked outside to join me on the porch and saw the tears in my eyes. "Oh, Kevin, everything will be okay," she tried to reassure me. "It will."

I stepped off the porch, and Kelena watched as my body tensed in the burning light of the sun. The tears that filled my eyes and the exposed hair of my body quickly burned away as ashes in the air. I clenched my teeth, taking a bit more pain before jumping back to the shade of the porch. I could only stand about seven seconds of sunlight. I bent over, putting my hands on my knees to steady myself. The sun was nauseating. My body shook from the pain. My blood boiled, and the pain receptors of my skin were all firing like tiny nuclear blasts!

"So that's how you stay so smooth and clean," Kelena commented with a little laugh to try cheering me up.

Kieran came outside to find me doubled over and breathing hard. "All right, what happened? I can't leave you two alone for a minute! Did you punch him in the stomach?"

"No," she answered, and I could almost hear her roll her eyes. "He decided to go sunbathing," she laughed. "Nothing purifies like fire, now does it?" she said to me, rubbing my head and helping me stand. My skin was extremely sensitive, so I winced beneath her touch.

"You haven't been feeding like you should," Kieran told me. "How long do you go between meals?"

"I don't know, maybe three days."

"Three days!"

"I'll get you something. Just hold on," Kelena told me, holding up a finger before vanishing to who knows where.

Kieran and I sat in the wrought iron chairs on my porch.

"I read your book," he said to me.

"Just now?" I asked, astounded.

"Yeah, it was decent. I think you exaggerated a bit here and there, and you excluded a lot, but overall, it wasn't bad."

"Thanks," I said in a dry, disheartened tone.

Shaking his head, "I didn't mean it that way," he apologized.

"I know. I know," I said, raising a hand to stop him. "It's okay. I'm fine."

The door opened suddenly, and Kelena stepped outside, putting a straw down into a bag of donated blood. Kieran and I looked at her, confused. She handed me the blood before taking a seat next to me. "I got you a whole mini fridge full of 'em," she finally said with a big smile.

"Aren't those for people in need of a trans-fusion?" Kieran questioned his sister.

"You know his body doesn't make blood," Kelena argued. "If anyone needs it, it's Kevin."

Taking a gulp through the straw, I thanked her.

"Oh," she said suddenly, pointing to the label on the bag. "This one's B+. Get it? Be positive." She couldn't contain herself. She cracked up from her own joke.

I almost got strangled from laughing. "That's pretty clever," I admitted.

Even Kieran found it amusing.

Already feeling better, I asked, "So what can we do to help Seraphine?"

"I think we should go kick ass," Kelena suggested, looking from me to Kieran for one of us to accept her plan.

"We'll go speak to Manius first," Kieran told her, laughing.

"This shouldn't take long," Kelena said to me with a grin, punching her hand, "but it would probably be best to wait till we get back before you message Seraphine."

"I don't want to sit around here and wait," I told them disappointedly. "You could forget about me and be gone a year like you were last time."

"We didn't forget you," Kelena responded. "There was just a lot to see. And we weren't gone an entire year. It was just a few months."

"So can I go?" I asked them.

Before Kieran could refuse, which I'm sure he would have, Kelena answered, "Of course you can go with us." Turning to her brother, she added, "I promise, I'll look after him." She too must have foreseen Kieran's answer.

"When do we leave?" I asked excitedly, ready for a trip.

"Grab your hoodie," Kieran told me while looking at his twin sister with disapproval.

I sucked down the last of my drink and ran inside to get my coat. I never know when I may be out in the sun, so it's always good to go prepared.

In my bedroom, I found the mini fridge that Kelena picked up for me. I opened it to find that it was indeed full of blood bags. I grabbed another drink and popped in a straw before rejoining the twins on the porch so we could leave. "Thought I'd grab one for the road," I told them.

"We won't be taking any roads," Kieran said with a grin.

CHAPTER II

OFFICE MEETING

In a bright flash of light, Kieran teleported the three of us to a hall in an office building. There were pictures of fighter jets, national monuments, and historical events along the hallway where we were standing, and the nearest office door name plate read "MANIUS MAGNUSON."

"Why does Manius have an office? Where are we?" I asked.

"We're at the Pentagon," he answered before knocking twice on the office door.

A stunning, Middle Eastern woman in a black dress opened the door with a smile. "Kieran, it's so good to see you," she greeted warmly, giving him a hug.

By the expression on his face, I could tell he had no clue who this woman was. "Um, good afternoon, ma'am."

"Kelena, I've always loved your strawberry curls," she commented, touching her hair and giving her a hug as well.

Kelena obviously didn't know her either and looked uncomfortable with this lady in her personal space.

"Congratulations on your ascension," she said to them.

"Excuse me?" Kelena asked. "Ascension?"

"Yes. You've ascended from the confines of your body. The ingredients that you were comprised of were forged within stars," the exotic woman explained, cupping her hands together. "When those ingredients broke down to the energy that fashioned them, you were able to hold yourself together by retaining that energy instead of it dissipating into the far reaches of space."

"Okay. I'm sorry I asked," Kelena commented, overwhelmed by the answer.

"So the elves were right!" Kieran exclaimed. "The Sun did give us life!"

"You had part of the equation correct," the woman informed him, "but you were far from solving it," she added with a smile before turning to me.

"And Kevin," she said, drawing me in for a warm embrace. "Baldness suits you, but don't you miss all that pretty, blond hair you used to have?"

"Sometimes," I admitted, "but most of the time, I like the extra clean feeling of being bald."

"Hair or no hair, you make a pretty boy," she said, touching me lightly on the shoulder. "Why isn't Seraphine with you?"

I didn't know how to answer her question, or if I should answer at all.

"I wanted to play matchmaker, so I arranged it so your paths would cross here in D.C.," she revealed. "She's such a wonderful girl."

"Well, that's partially the reason I'm here," I began to explain.

Putting our conversation on hold, she welcomed us into the office. "Please come in, and we'll get this all worked out. Manius has been expecting you."

We followed her into the large office, and the charming woman closed the door behind us.

Manius stood from his desk chair and walked over greet us. "Kieran, it's good to see you again, my old friend," he outstretched a hand for him to shake.

Within a blink, Kieran held Manius by the throat in the sunlight shining through the office windows! "It was you!" Kieran yelled. "You orchestrated everything to get my power and have me do your dirty work!"

Kelena took my hand and positioned herself between me and Manius' secretary, but she didn't act hostile towards us at all. In fact, the woman sat calmly on the edge of the desk and watched as Manius remained helpless under Kieran's interrogation.

"I should hold you here in the sun until you burn to ashes!" Kieran threatened furiously.

Manius tried to speak but could only murmur within Kieran's choking grasp. Kieran pulled him close, anger burning hot in his eyes, but he took a deep breath and released him.

Manius dropped to the floor, coughing and scrambling to get out of the sunlight pouring through the window. "Destroy the body, and you'll unleash the fire," he warned with a laugh.

"It's time you tell me everything," Kieran

ordered.

"Of course," Manius submitted, smoothing out his suit and straightening his tie. Kieran watched him closely as he returned to his desk. The hair on the back of his head was burned away by the afternoon sun.

From the office entrance, there were large windows on the far wall looking out into the center courtyard of the complex. The thick curtains were open, but sunlight didn't reach Manius' desk, which was positioned along the right wall. Behind his desk was a bookshelf that was filled with normal looking books. None of the décor seemed strange or inhuman for that matter. There was a very nice topographical globe in the far corner, next to his desk. There was also a leather couch and two leather chairs surrounding a small, round table to the left of the windows. A large LCD TV hung in the corner to the left of the entrance. He had three chairs in front of his desk, almost like they were there for us. His unusual secretary did say that he was expecting us. She stood and walked to the far end of the desk and sat down. The desk was large enough to accommodate him and still have room for her at the end where her chair was stationed.

Manius motioned to the three chairs saying, "Please, if you will, have a seat. I have much to tell you. It seems this meeting has been delayed for far too long."

Kieran nodded to his sister that it was okay.

"Come on, Kevin," Kelena whispered and led me to sit in the chair closest to the door. She took the middle seat, and Kieran sat nearest to Manius' secretary.

His desk was kept clean and neat. Manius and his secretary each had a laptop computer, a cell phone, and a desk phone. There were also a couple file baskets with papers in them and a small digital clock.

"Before we begin, I'd like to introduce you to my lovely wife, Vistilia," Manius said with an affectionate smile.

She sat poised and proper as if basking in Manius' compliment.

Amazed, Kieran asked, "So you're the one who started all this? You made Manius the first vampire? How?"

"I am the one," she graciously admitted. "Keep in mind there were many types of vampires already in existence long before Manius," she explained. "He was merely the first of his kind. As for the question of how, I think you should let him tell his journey first." With that, she glanced at me with a knowing smile.

She must've read my book, I thought to myself.

"Ah yes, Kevin's book," Manius spoke. He held up his hand, and a copy of my book magically slid from the shelf behind him and floated to his waiting hand. "Immortal Journey by Kevin D. Blackmon," he read aloud. He placed it on the desk and spun it around so that it was facing right-side-up to us. "A nonfiction book written as fiction; clever. I prefer the works of Tolkien myself, but this wasn't a bad read," he admitted.

"I'm not the greatest writer; I don't claim to be," I spoke out in defense. "I wrote Kieran's tale the best I could and released it to the world because I think it's a good story."

Kelena clapped; she was proud that I stood up for myself.

"It is a wonderful story, Kevin," Vistilia com-plimented.

Kieran leaned forward in his chair to say, "And

I am truly honored that your first book told my story. Thank you."

"Yes. Well, I told you it wasn't bad, so don't worry yourself," Manius said. "Your skill as a writer isn't the reason I'm bringing this to your attention."

"It's about Seraphine," I told him, clasping my hands together, so they wouldn't shake quite so much. "I love her, and I'm afraid something may have happened to her. She left because I drew too much unwanted attention. I released my book as fiction, but there are real monsters still out there, and they know that I wrote the truth. They've attacked me and swore that I will know pain for breaking their law."

"Yes," Manius acknowledged with a smirk. "The irrefutable existence of an old world race must never be exposed."

Kelena reached over and took hold of my shaking hands to calm me.

"You no doubt have realized your mistake in writing about your girlfriend," Manius said to me, "but again, that isn't the reason I'm bringing this to your attention. What you all have failed to realize is, by writing your little story," he said, picking up the book and shaking it in front of us, "you've also drawn attention to me and other creatures that were thought to reside only in folktales. Investigations have opened. Documented sightings of strange creatures are being reexamined. Most of the old races have been completely extinguished, but there are still many shapeshifters, vampires and other undead that should remain hidden from the public eye. Imagine how fast news would spread in this technological age if someone caught on video one of these creatures or one of us, for that matter.

How do you think the world would react?"

"Chaotic," Kieran thought aloud.

"Yes, not to mention what today's scientists could learn if they got their hands on an actual tome of magic or an artifact imbued with arcane power," Manius added.

"Do you think human scientists would be able to cast spells?" Kieran asked.

"Humans are persistent and resourceful," he answered. "They will find a way. Even if they have to become a vampire like Kevin here, they will do whatever is necessary."

"But, if humans open the door to the arcane and that power falls into the wrong hands, all life could be destroyed!" Kieran told us.

"Yes, it could," Manius agreed.

"What is it you would like us to do?" Kelena asked, growing impatient. "The book is out. The damage has already been done."

"You're right, there is no going back," Manius admitted. "I don't see this as irrefutable proof of mythical creatures," he clarified, tapping on my book, "but obviously, it was enough to open some eyes. With your popularity on the rise," he said to me, "people will soon realize that you really are what you say you are. So I've decided I want you to write my story."

"What?" the three of us asked in unison, questioning our hearing.

"Continue to market your books as fiction, so to not alarm the general reader," Manius began to explain, handing me an ink pen. "You know, life could be a lot worse. Everyone should be thankful the dragons no longer rule," he said, opening a desk drawer to get a legal pad for me to write on.

"How could releasing another book possibly help?" Kelena asked.

"I fear that my time here is coming to an end, and I don't want the life that I've lived to go unheard," Manius answered sadly.

"Don't give us that!" Kieran blurted out. "You cannot die. You are immortal, just like us."

"Do not take for granted the power you believe you hold over Death, for he may surprise you."

"What do you mean?" Kieran asked.

"Nothing is certain," he answered plainly.

"And that still doesn't explain how writing a book about you will help the situation!" Kelena told him.

"No, it doesn't, my dear," Manius answered, "but everything will work itself out."

"Of all people, how can you say that?" Kieran asked. "Your plan from the beginning was to mold the world as you see fit because you didn't think it would turn in man's favor. You've eradicated entire races and erased them from history to see your plan through."

"Yes, that was my plan, and it is nearly complete. I'm not especially proud of what I've done, but trust me when I say it's what needed to happen to protect this world from total destruction. Here," he said, handing me a pad of paper. "You may want to take notes; I have quite the story to tell."

ACT II

2322 BC

CHAPTER III

YOUNG AND STRONG FOREVER

My story begins just before dawn on the day of my death. I was lying in a candle lit room. My beloved wife, Vistilia, sat next to me with my hand in hers to ease my passing. She pressed a wet towel against my forehead, and I felt the cool water trickle through my thinning, grey hair.

"You have been by my side through the hard times and through the great," I told her with a weak, raspy voice. "I couldn't have asked for a better wife or a better friend."

"You speak as if you're leaving me," she said with a genuine smile.

"I am 54 years old. I have been sick for more than a month."

"Fifty-four years is not old," she commented.

I coughed out a laugh. "I have already outlived

most people. I feel I will not live through the night."

"Even if you outlived the oldest of stars, it would still be too short of a life."

Her strange words always brought me an odd sense of comfort. "But I wouldn't want to live such a long life without you by my side," I confessed.

"And what would you do with your life if you and I were to live forever?" she asked.

"I would want us to have the children that we never had, and I would want to protect them and everyone's children from the monsters that dwell outside our city's borders." My grip tightened over her hand as I fought to hold on.

With a calm, soothing voice, Vistilia told me, "Then wish it. Wish for what needs to be, my love."

I gazed upon my beloved wife for what would've been the last time and noticed that she didn't show any sign of sadness. Her face was serene. Her eyes were dry, but I did not question her lack of grief. I used my dying breaths to tell her my wish. "I want us to be rid of these old and feeble bodies, to be young and strong forever." My vision blurred, and my open eyes became lifeless orbs.

Like from a fairytale, a kiss awakened me, and I drew breath again! I wiped coins from my eyes to find myself in an unfamiliar place. I was lying on a stone slab in a torch lit chamber. Vistilia waited patiently for me to get up, but she seemed different in the flickering torchlight. She appeared rejuvenated! I sat up from my resting place and breathed in the stale, cold air of the room before making my way to her. I was awestruck as

I caressed silky smooth skin that I'd not felt in years. She wore a white dress hemmed in gold, and her dark, olive skin was radiantly perfect.

"My love, you are young again!" I finally spoke with tears welling up in my eyes at the sight of her.

"We are young again," she corrected me, taking my face in both hands to kiss me. She then made a circular motion in the air to create a mirror in the space before me, so I could see that I too appeared young.

Not only was I amazed that we appeared in our 20s again, but she was able to create a mirror from thin air! Until now, I had no clue she had any kind of magical ability. I watched myself touch my face, and I was suddenly afraid. "What has happened?" I asked, turning away from my reflection. "Where are we?"

"You died," she answered bluntly, waving the mirror away.

"I what?"

"Died," she repeated. "And then I granted your wish," she added nonchalantly, walking away to watch a spider wrap a moth.

I paused for a moment as the truth of the situation sank in. "Couldn't you have granted my wish just a little sooner?"

Vistilia laughed at my question. "Well, you needed to be dead, so your wish could be fulfilled without drawing attention."

She began fixing the spider's tattered web, filling in the broken areas with strings of silk that seemed to originate from the tip of her finger.

"Your ties to the mortal world must be severed," she continued. "You cannot reveal to the world that you are different, or you will not be welcome."

"How is this possible?" I asked, stepping closer to watch her finish repairing the web. "How are you doing this? I've known you my entire life and never knew you had such power."

The spider seemed unaware of her assistance as it returned to the center of the large, round web.

"You may have known me your entire life, but I am far older in this world than you think," she confessed.

"And I thought I knew everything about you." I kissed her bare shoulder and looked toward the stone slab where I awoke. "How long was I dead?"

"Eight days," she answered, turning to face me.

I was speechless for a moment as I stared at what was to be my final resting place. "There was nothing," I finally said. "There was no ferryman to carry me across the river. There were no gods to welcome me to the afterlife. If I had not awakened, I would have never known that I had ever existed." Vistilia embraced me, and I stared blankly at my stone bed from over her shoulder. "I would face all the tortures of the gods to not see that again," I told her.

Running her fingers through my hair, she kissed me. Her skin was silky soft. Her long, raven hair glistened in the torchlight.

We pulled away slowly, and my focus returned to the many questions that I must ask. "So are you going to tell me how you're able to do all this?"

"I will," she assured me with a smile. "But first, we need to get you a drink."

Confusion fell over me, and she took my hand, leading me out of the burial chamber. We walked through the moonlit city. I noticed my senses sharpening. My vision became clearer, and I could hear bats catching bugs in the air above.

Suddenly, my stomach cramped, and I doubled over in pain. "I've gone too long without eating?" I told her as she helped me stand.

"I know you're hungry," she said to me, "but the food you ate in your previous life will not sustain you now."

She led me to the front door of not our house but someone else's. "Why are we here?" I asked.

The door seemed to open on its own as she gestured for me to enter. I hesitantly walked inside, and the door closed quietly behind us. Vistilia walked around me and through the house. There was a large table covered in drawings of mountains, forests, towns, and rivers on papyrus.

"This is the map maker's home. Where are you going?" I whispered, but she didn't answer. Feeling uncomfortable about breaking in like this, I reluctantly followed her. I found her in the bedroom standing over the sleeping man and his wife. I silently walked up to Vistilia to whisper in her ear. "We don't belong here. Let's leave before we wake them."

"Only fresh blood will sustain you now," she explained.

I looked at her in disbelief, but before I could say another word, I doubled over with hunger pangs again. The pain was excruciating, but I was able to keep my growls to a minimum and right myself. "What have you done to me?" I whispered strongly.

"You are exactly as you should be," she answered with a sly smile.

I looked back at the sleeping couple.

"You need not kill them," she assured me. "You need only to take a little from both to satisfy your hunger."

"How can I take a drink without waking them?" I asked.

"Think about what you need to do before you do it."

I stared at the couple, taking a moment to think. I then glanced around at their bedchamber. It was nicely furnished with pictures on the walls and two bureaus. On one of the bureaus, I saw a small dagger that I could use. I punched the man and then the woman. "They should be out for a few minutes." I used the dagger to make a small slit in the bend of the man's arm. As blood began to flow from the cut, I was hesitant to put my mouth to it. I looked at Vistilia, but she said nothing. I touched my tongue to the blood. I was not impressed with the initial taste but tried a bit more. Surprisingly, the more I drank, the more I liked it. I soon began seeing visions, glimpses of maps and roads to cities. I heard his heartbeat quicken, and it frightened me. I released the man in fear that I would kill him.

Licking my lips, my tongue caught on my canine teeth. That's when I noticed they had gotten longer. I looked at the unconscious woman and used my extended canines to pierce the skin of her arm. With her, I could feel that she was happy with her husband. She was happy with their life in Athens, and she was ready to have children. I drank until I heard her heartbeat flutter before pulling myself away. The two small punctures left by my canines were not bleeding as badly as the cut I made on her husband.

"Ah, much better," I said aloud with a look of

satisfaction. I walked over to my beautiful wife, and with her back against the wall, I kissed her, sharing the blood that remained on my lips. "We should get out of here before they regain consciousness."

Before leaving, I took down a framed picture that hung over their bed and laid it on the unconscious couple, so they would think that was the reason they were bruised and cut. Once outside, I began to walk toward our home.

"We can't go home," Vistilia told me.

Remembering that I'd been dead for more than a week, I understood. "I suppose it wouldn't do for people to see that I've risen from the grave, but what about you? What about us?"

"I died too," she revealed. "I couldn't grant your wish, then send you away on your own. I appeared to die from blood loss."

In shock, I was speechless.

"No bite marks," she clarified. "After finding you dead, I felt I couldn't go on living, so I slit my wrists. With no children or family for our house and possessions to go to, they went to the king. All we have are the clothes we're wearing," she admitted with a smile.

With a heavy sigh, I said nothing.

"We can no longer stay here," she said, walking around to the side of the house. "Come on. We'll take these two horses and head out of town."

Hesitant to steal something else from the map maker, I did as she commanded. We took his horses, and I led the way out of town. We traveled road after road, riding through the night.

"We're heading to Thebes, but I've never been

to Thebes," I told Vistilia, who was following close behind. I slowed my horse for us to ride side by side. "How do I know the way?"

"Other than a resistance to disease and old age, I've given you the power to read people's thoughts. The power is strongest when you feed on someone," she explained. "All of their thoughts and memories are yours to take."

"So I not only took some of the map maker's blood but his knowledge of other cities as well," I thought aloud.

The morning sun began to break through the trees. I winced every time a beam of sunlight hit my skin. "Why does the light hurt me?"

"I think life would be very boring if you didn't have obstacles to overcome," she answered.

I slowed my horse and maneuvered into the shadows of the trees.

"You have already felt your thirst for blood. Your weakness to sunlight is but another obstacle," Vistilia continued.

I brought my right hand up so a beam of sunlight shining through the forest would hit it. I held it there for a few short seconds and watched it begin to singe and smoke. When I could bear the searing pain no longer, I pulled my hand away. "Why? Why this?" I asked.

"You must have limitations," she explained. "Since you cannot die of natural causes, there must be equally difficult obstacles."

Even lightly rubbing my sunburned hand caused me to wince beneath the pain. "Do I have any other weaknesses or limitations that I should be aware of?"

"You may be immortal, but you're not indestructible," she answered. "You must protect your brain at all costs. It is what's needed to exist. If your brain is damaged beyond repair, the thoughts and memories that make you who you are will be lost. You will be gone."

"Well, can't you just bring me back?" I asked, but she didn't answer. "I thought you said you couldn't let me go out on my own? I sense you're leaving me."

"I'm sorry Manius, but I can't physically be with you every step of the way. We will part for some time, but you needn't worry about that now." She turned her horse to continue down the trail.

"But why me? Why turn me into this? Why extend my life indefinitely?" I asked, not ready to move on without more answers. "And you still haven't told me how it is that you have such power?"

Vistilia halted her horse and turned to face me. She vanished in an instant only to reappear sitting behind me on my horse with her arms wrapped tightly around me. "My dear Manius, my love, we have so much ahead of us. I promise, I will tell you everything when you are ready."

"When I'm ready?" I asked, turning to see her head on my shoulder.

"Many paths lie ahead. You only need to choose which to take when you come to them. You are a wonderful man. I've loved my life with you, and we have many exciting adventures ahead."

With merely a nod, I agreed to be patient.

A smile broke across her face, and she gave me a quick kiss on the cheek before magically returning to her horse. "And besides," she began to say, "if I reveal too much, it will ruin the fun!" With that, her horse reared up and leaped into a full gallop. Her laughter rang out, and I followed as quickly as my horse would carry me down the woodland trail. My own laughter could no longer be contained.

CHAPTER IV

MORTAL AND IMMORTAL LIFE

As we rode, I passed through beams of sunlight only long enough to singe the hair on my arms. I had a feeling that my new life would be quite different from my previous one, and I began thinking back on it.

I was born in the city of Atronos in 2376 BC on the island of Crete. A week after my birth, a Persian woman found her way to our city. She was pregnant and ready to give birth. My father aided with the painful delivery, and the woman said the baby was to be named Vistilia. With her dying breaths, she left her newborn daughter in my father's care.

Like most boys, I began learning the art of combat at an early age. With my father being our greatest hero, I was proud to have the greatest teacher.

He and our city guards protected us for many years. That is, until the Sea Giants set their greedy eyes upon our land. My father died defending us, and the city erected a statue in honor of him.

After his death, my mother became an active speaker for the city planning. Our council was made up of elders, but they always welcomed fresh new ideas from the younger generation, and my mother's voice was a strong one. She gave them many great ideas before she died of fever when I was 15.

The following year, I was old enough to join the city guard, so I followed in my father's footsteps. With his courage and my mother's resourcefulness, I quickly became the city's new champion. In just a few short years, I had helped establish peace between the surrounding settlements. I trained soldiers and helped build outposts in strategic locations. I not only protected my own city from hordes of strange creatures, I also helped strengthen our allies' defenses.

Unlike my mother, Vistilia never got involved with the decision making of the city council, and I didn't pressure her to do so. She was content with staying home and maintaining a productive garden. We always had more food than the two of us could eat, so she often traded baskets of freshly picked fruits and vegetables at the market square.

We lived in our family's house for many years. Growing up as best friends, we never felt we needed anyone else, and our love for one another grew with us into adulthood. Of course, I was disappointed to learn that she was unable to bear children, but I loved her no less.

One night in the year 2350, I was awakened by screams! I grabbed my sword and ran out into the city streets to find that the Sea Giants had returned, and this time, they had a much larger army. The ground shook with the thundering steps of the hulking, human-like creatures, and the air was filled with the screams of people being crushed beneath them. No doubt, the guards stationed at the city outposts were killed before they could signal that we were under attack.

Through the thick of chaos, my beloved Vistilia made her way to me in the streets where I was gathering a few troops to take back the city. "Manius, you cannot win this battle," she cried. "We must flee while we're still able."

I looked at the city burning and crumbling around us. "But I have a duty to..."

"You won't be much good to your people if you die here tonight," she argued. "Manius, my love," she said, taking hold of my hand, "please, you've done all you can do to defend Atronos, but you are hopelessly outmatched."

I had never seen her so afraid. I agreed to retreat, not to save myself, but to make sure she got to safety. I ordered my fellow soldiers to get their families out of the city, and with giants smashing through buildings and anyone in their path, I led Vistilia between burning houses. We made our way to the edge of the city unseen and ran down to the docks where we took a small boat out to sea. It was painful to watch the city my family sacrificed so much for burning as Vistilia and I escaped toward the mainland.

"I've failed you, father!" I cried out to the darkness. "I've failed our people."

Vistilia held me as I broke down and sobbed.

We were at sea for a week before reaching Athens. The name of Manius preceded me, but I was unable to mobilize a force large enough to challenge the giants. I wanted to go back to see the fate of Atronos, but Vistilia convinced me to stay with her in Athens.

"It is too dangerous to go back unprepared," she said to me.

I had to accept that the city of Atronos was no more.

For the next few years, I continued to train soldiers, and at 35, I was elected to take a seat among the Athenian council. By that time, news had reached my ears that Atronos had indeed been utterly destroyed.

"The Sea Giants are using Atronos as a foothold with plans to conquer all of Crete," I presented to the king and the Athenian council. "We cannot lose Crete to these monsters, for their sights may next be upon mother Greece itself."

My argument was enough to get approval for a full scale assault, but because of my position on the council, I could not go to war. I had to stay behind and impatiently wait a month for the first report to come in. We sent an army of 5,000 Greeks across the sea to defeat the giants and fortify the island. Five ships returned, carrying 137 men. The mission was a failure.

A soldier's words painted a terrible picture for the king and his council. "Following the will of the king," he began with a bow, "we divided our force a full day before reaching Crete. The small number of ships approaching the island from the north never reached land; they were swallowed by the sea. The rest of the fleet reached the eastern shore only to face an army we were not prepared to face. We found that the Sea Giants had allied themselves with the Storm Giants to capture Crete and enslave its people."

Dismissing the soldier, the king and his council discussed the next step. Servant girls brought wine and fruit, for it was going to be a long day.

"We must gather an even bigger army to send to Crete," a council member suggested.

"What if it's still not enough?" another asked. "The Storm Giants are an even fiercer race than the Sea Giants, capable of calling on the power of Zeus to strike their enemies."

The king spoke, "It seems that the mighty Zeus has already decided who will rule the Mediterranean and has chosen the giants. We must accept the god's decision."

"What if it's a test?" I asked. Before anyone could answer, I continued. "What if Zeus is testing us to see if we are worthy of ruling the Mediterranean?"

"It seems we have failed that test, Manius," the king stated.

"No," I responded sternly. The room fell silent, shocked at my manners toward our king. "I may have lost Atronos, but I can rebuild it. I will not lose Crete. We," I stressed, "cannot afford to lose Crete because, if we lose Crete, we lose the Mediterranean and what next? We must prove ourselves to Zeus and the other gods that humans are worthy to rule. We must prove that we will never give up!"

The king didn't seem angered but impressed with me. "What do you propose we do?" he asked.

"We explain the situation to the rulers of the Mediterranean lands, and by combining their soldiers, we will have an army that will make even the giants tremble."

Approving the plan, the king sent word to the

surrounding kingdoms, but we couldn't rally the number of troops needed, and we learned that giants weren't the only monsters threatening mankind. There was nothing we could do but rebuild our army and keep safe the citizens of Athens.

A scent in the air stirred me from my thoughts. I stopped my horse and raised a hand to signal Vistilia to stop. I listened for a moment and heard growling nearby. I dismounted my horse and followed the sound to find a pack of wolves feeding on a deer.

"Walk on out there, honey," Vistilia said to me with a smile. She had quietly followed me into the woods.

"Are you crazy?" I whispered. "They'll tear me apart!"

"Oh, you'll be fine," she tried to assure me. "You're smarter than they are."

"It would be smart of me to leave them alone."

She gave me a nudge and told me, "Watch their movements and show no fear. You'll be all right."

I walked slowly toward the pack of five wolves and their meal. They turned their attention to me and growled. I continued toward them, showing my open palms that I came peacefully.

"Easy now," I said soothingly. "I just want a taste."

Their growls grew louder. I didn't believe it was a good idea to disturb them, especially during their lunch. Two of the wolves suddenly charged me! I backhanded one into the other, knocking them away. One leaped at my face, but I punched it in the side of the head, fracturing its skull. I backhanded another wolf into a tree, breaking its spine. I'm much faster and stronger now than before I died, I thought to myself.

Being more cautious, the remaining wolf began to circle me. It growled and snarled, but I turned its scare tactics against itself. I let out a loud roar, and it cowered away from me. As it turned to run, I quickly snatched it up and sank my fangs in. Unable to move, I squeezed the helpless wolf tighter and tighter, crushing the life from it until I drained every drop of its blood.

While I drank, the first two wolves that attacked me escaped. I tossed the remains of my lunch to the ground and noticed the wolf fur of my hands. As I wiped the fur away, the softness of breathing drew my attention. I could see the warmth emanating from three small creatures in bushes nearby.

A dart came at me from one of the bushes! I dodged it but two others struck me! One of them stuck into my thigh, the other into my neck. I quickly pulled the darts from my skin and cast them aside. I felt a burning sensation around the wounds, but it quickly faded.

"Show yourselves!" I yelled at them.

The creatures ran from me. I pushed through the bushes and caught a glimpse of them hopping away like deer but with only two legs. They were fast, but I was able catch up to them in a forest grove where they were using a fallen tree as a bridge to cross a stream.

I knocked one of the creatures to the ground and held it down while it thrashed and bellowed.

"What kind of creature are you?" I asked, but it was obviously too wild to understand me. It only struggled to free itself.

It was about three feet tall with hock jointed hind legs and covered in short, black fur. It held a reed pipe that it had used to blow poisoned darts. Its face appeared almost human beneath its hair, but it had pointy ears and antlers on top of its head resembling a goat.

I could feel its frightened blood coursing beneath the surface of its skin, and I was drawn to it. I was about to bite into the creature when one of the others butted me with its horns to push me away from its kin.

There were dozens of the diminutive creatures here, and they seemed angry that I was trespassing on their territory. One by one, the creatures charged at me, but I pushed them harmlessly away.

"Careful now," I laughed. "Someone could get hurt."

I was then hit with many poison tipped darts from their blowguns!

"Ouch." The poison had no ill effect on me but, all those darts at once, stung. I didn't have time to pull them out, so I continued defending myself from the creatures.

A horn was blown to halt the attack on me, and with the aid of a cane, their leader stepped out on a large, moss-covered rock that overlooked the stream. His hair was all white, and he had a long, wispy beard that hung to his hoofed feet. I noticed that the older members of this woodland race had less facial hair, so they appeared more humanlike.

"You create imbalance here," the old creature said to me in a scruffy voice.

"Imbalance?" I repeated, looking up at him. "I don't understand. What do you mean?"

"You disrupt the cycle of life," he answered.

"Who are you?"

"I am Jur-Jon of the Fauns, but that is a question you should ask yourself?"

I was taken aback by his reversal of the question.

"You must leave," he ordered. "You do not belong here."

Glancing around, I saw that there were dozens of fauns ready to defend their territory. Many of their blowguns were already set on me. "Very well," I agreed. "I will leave peacefully." I then began backing slowly out of the grove.

Yes, this life was definitely different, I thought to myself before backing into Vistilia. I hadn't noticed she was still with me.

"And this is only the beginning," she admitted, clearly reading my thoughts. Peering through the undergrowth at the fauns in the forest grove, she added sweetly, "Aww! Look what cute little creatures you've discovered."

"If you want to go pet them, be my guest," I suggested with a laugh. "Look what those cute little creatures did to me," I told her, pointing at the many poison-tipped darts embedded in my flesh.

Laughing, she said, "Don't be such a baby. Those things aren't big enough to really hurt you."

Watching me carefully pluck a dart from my cheek, she said, "Here, let me help you with those."

"That one went all the way through," I told her as my tongue felt the wound inside my mouth.

After she helped remove the darts that littered my body, we walked back to our horses and continued on to the city of Thebes.

KEVIN D. BLACKMON

CHAPTER V

A CHANGE OF CLOTHING

We reached Thebes after dark and left our horses outside the city. Tired of animals, I thirsted for human blood and quickly spotted a guard patrolling the city.

"Be careful; you don't want to cause a panic," Vistilia warned. "Even though you are more powerful, it doesn't mean they cannot make your existence difficult."

Taking note, I snuck silently into the city, keeping my eyes on my prey. The guard was carrying a torch in one hand and a short spear in the other. He was wearing leather armor but no helmet.

I crouched in the shadows between two buildings and began scratching one of the building walls loud enough to get the guard's attention as he passed by. The guard looked between the buildings, but it was too dark for his eyes to see what was making the noise. I eased farther back, continuing to scratch the stone. The guard readied his spear and cautiously walked between the buildings. I eased my way around the back and scratched a little more before I stopped and waited.

He listened for a moment, but all that could be heard now were the cicadas. He breathed in deeply and looked around the back of the building where the scratching noise came from, but nothing was there. He turned quickly to look behind the other building, but it too was clear. Before he could exhale a sigh of relief, I locked my arms around his neck. Dropping his torch and spear, he tried futilely to escape. I forced him to the ground and felt the fight leave him as he went unconscious.

"I'm sorry, friend, but you have something that I need," I said to him before my fangs pierced the skin, and his life poured into me.

He was young, not twenty years of age. He married his childhood sweetheart last winter and planned to have children soon.

I released him from my bite. "You have a long life ahead, and I'm not here to take it from you," I whispered to the unconscious city watchman. I turned to rejoin Vistilia outside the city's boundaries but was startled to find her standing behind me.

"Very good, sweetheart," Vistilia congratulated me.

"Shhh," I quieted her. "Let's stay near our horses outside of town until dawn. Then we can go indoors."

She placed a finger over her lips and skipped to a large oak tree within view of the city. I sat with her, our backs against the tree.

"I think I'd like to have an apple," she said aloud.

I laughed because it was an odd craving to have at such an early hour.

At the snap of her fingers, the oak became an apple tree, and an apple dropped to her waiting hand! She took a large bite and kissed my cheek. "I love an apple for breakfast," she said with a giggle.

What does a person say when they witness a miracle? When it concerns the unexplainable, do words really hold any meaning? Even the small act of turning acorns to apples is beyond comprehension.

"Look out there," Vistilia pointed, with apple in hand, to the stars. "I put those there for you. The night sky would be quite dull without stars."

"Are you a god?" I finally asked.

She smiled, taking another bite of the apple. "I am here," she answered while chewing. "But I am no different from anyone else, where I'm from," she added, laying her head on my shoulder and finishing her apple.

"I know where you are from. You were born in Atronos, but I don't understand how you acquired all this power."

"This body that I inhabit was born in Atronos," she clarified.

"Do you mean that you're really from out there?" I asked, pointing up.

"I am from . . . elsewhere," she answered, giving me a quick kiss on the cheek.

The stars faded with the coming dawn, so we gathered our horses and led them into the city.

As soon as businesses began opening, Vistilia and I stepped into a clothing store. I had only one set of clothing, and I had been wearing them for over a week in a crypt, so you could imagine they weren't in the best of condition.

"Good morning," the shopkeeper greeted us. "My name is Tabitha. Welcome to my shop."

"Good morning," we responded as we began looking over the clothes she had neatly displayed on tables.

She came over and picked out a dark red tunic and black cloak. She held them up to me to get an idea of what I would look like wearing them.

"Oh, you will look great in those," Vistilia commented.

"You're welcome to try them on behind the shade, if you like," Tabitha said, handing me the clothes.

I took them and stepped behind the changing shade.

"There is a wash basin, a towel, and a comb back there so feel free to clean up," the shopkeeper told me.

"Can you pick him out a pair of black sandals and a matching belt?" Vistilia asked her.

"I can," she answered before hurrying away.

Vistilia looked over the store, noticing how neat and clean it was kept.

Tabitha returned, handing a pair of sandals and a belt around the shade for me to take. She then stood with Vistilia, and they waited for me to step out.

"He really needed a new outfit," Vistilia told her. "We have just moved here from Athens, and we didn't have any way to carry both his clothes and mine. And, you know, a woman always has to look good."

The two ladies laughed.

"I'm glad you chose to come to my shop," I

heard the shopkeeper tell Vistilia. "Alexander, the owner of the clothing shop across the street, sends people to get my prices on things, so he can price his just a bit lower. He has gone so far as letting rats loose in my shop to tear up my clothes to make their nests. He wants to be the only clothing shop in the city. That is why he opened across the street from me."

"Is there anything we can do to help you?" Vistilia asked.

"I don't think there is anything that can be done within the law," she answered, "and I don't believe in fighting dirty like he does. Thank you for the offer though."

"Did you report him for setting rats loose in your shop?"

"I did, but of course, there was no way I could prove that he did it because of a hole found in the corner of my shop."

From behind the shade, I could see freshly packed clay at the bottom of the back wall.

"I know that he knocked that hole in my wall," I heard her continue. "I know it, but I cannot prove it."

"What do men know about style anyway?" Vistilia commented, and they both burst into laughter.

I stepped out from behind the shade, wearing the new clothes and the cloak thrown over my shoulder. The two ladies stopped laughing. They were speechless at the sight of me. I was perfectly clean and handsome. Their stares brought a smile to my face. "So, how do I look?"

"Wow," Vistilia voiced her approval.

"It is definitely you," Tabitha responded.

"Good, because I like it," I told them.

Tabitha stepped behind the counter for a bag. "I'm going to give you this to carry your dirty clothes in, and I will give you a good deal on the whole outfit." She retrieved my tattered clothes from behind the shade. "I will only charge you twelve drachmas."

"That is a very good price. Thank you," I told her as Vistilia paid the nice lady.

"No. Thank you. I love knowing that I have the power to help someone's inner beauty shine brightly through their physical beauty."

"Thank you very much for your help," Visitilia added.

Before stepping out into the morning sun, I put my cloak on and pulled the hood up.

"I look forward to your return," the shopkeeper told us as we left, obviously showing off to Alexander that she had customers while he was standing outside his store.

Vistilia and I walked arm in arm throughout the city until nightfall.

When the night patrolmen were out of sight, I forced the door open to Alexander's Fine Clothing, breaking the lock with hardly any effort. With only a small amount of moonlight shining through the windows, I had to rely mostly on my newly gifted night vision to navigate the interior of the store. I walked around the counter and found a cask of beer behind a curtain with several mugs. I also found a short sword that he no doubt kept for protection.

"Alexander doesn't need this kind of weapon," I said aloud as I strapped it to my side.

Just then, a light passed by the window, and I unsheathed the sword.

"Manius!" Vistilia whispered as she hid behind a table of folded clothes.

I silently moved behind the door. It opened quickly, and a guard ran inside ready to fight off any thieves. I struck him in the head with the pommel of my sword, and the guard fell just as fast as he came in.

Vistilia ran over, shut the door, and blew out the torch that the guard was carrying. "What are we going to do with him?"

Sheathing the stolen sword, I took a deep breath. I cracked the door a bit to see if any more guards were coming. I heard footsteps approaching. I took a step back and prepared myself to knock out another guard. A man in his nightwear, carrying a candle, slowly pushed the door open. He saw the guard on the floor, but before he could call for help, I knocked him out. I shut the door and turned the man over to see that it was Alexander.

"What are we going to do now?" Vistilia asked.

Looking around the room, I began formulating a plan.

At dawn, a guard noticed that Alexander's shop door was cracked open. He slowly pushed the door open and saw an unconscious man, tied belly-down over the counter, wearing women's clothing. Alexander was unconscious, lying on the floor, wearing the guard's armor with a mug in his hand. Beer had poured out onto the floor, and there were empty mugs scattered about. The guard that had found them looked a little sickened and shocked for only a moment before he started to giggle and laugh. He stepped outside and waved over another guard to come examine the scene.

Vistilia and I stood in a crowd that was gathering outside the store. People were curious what happened during the night.

The city guards and even their captain came to investigate. Gasps and snickers from the growing crowd were heard as the guard, dressed in women's clothing, walked out rubbing his head. Seeing his captain, he stood at attention.

"What in the name of Zeus have you been doing, son?" the captain yelled.

"I don't know what happened, sir," the guard began. "I noticed the door to Alexander's shop was open, so I stepped inside. That is all I remember."

Alexander stepped out of his shop, still wearing the guard's armor. He too was rubbing his head.

The captain of the guards took a moment to look over what the night watchman and Alexander were wearing before commenting. "Now, you see what happens when you go in somewhere alone?" he asked aloud. He gestured toward Alexander with an open hand. "Alexander here has his way with you."

The townspeople and the guards laughed. The captain wanted to laugh but held it back as best he could.

"But I was knocked out too," Alexander spoke up. "I was awakened by noise from my shop, so I came over. I saw him lying in the floor, and then I was hit over the head. I never saw who hit me."

"Neither of you saw anyone inside the shop?" the captain asked.

Both men shook their heads.

"How convenient," he remarked, throwing his hands up and rolling his eyes. "You want to know what I see here? I see a guard who was in the wrong place at the wrong time, and a shop keeper whose thirst for brew put him in the mood for some fun." The captain looked over the guard once more. "And get out of that dress! You look like a damn fool!"

The guard captain turned to us and said, "All right, this little pageant is over. Go about your daily nothings."

As everyone began leaving the scene, Vistilia declared, "I think I could go for a cold beer."

"Cold?"

I walked with her to a tavern where she ordered a beer. Of course, I didn't order anything because I already had something to drink that day. After she took a swallow of her beer, she told me to take hold of it.

I held the mug as she said and was shocked that it was frosted over. Without thinking, I turned it up but gagged from the taste. After spitting beer in the floor, I told her, "It tastes like piss, but it's cold!"

"I prefer my beer cold, so I made it cold," she explained simply. She then began laughing to herself. "I doubt Alexander will be enjoying a beer anytime soon either," she said.

"News of Alexander's after-hour activities should hurt his business quite a bit," I commented.

"He will probably move across town, so he won't be so close to his competition," Vistilia added.

"And it may take some time to build his customer base back to what it was. That was fun!" I told her with a laugh.

"Perhaps now, Tabitha can run a successful business without someone trying to ruin it."

The barmaid walked over to check on us. She was a young girl, maybe seventeen years of age. She was plain but pretty with brown eyes and fair skin. She had long, brown hair, but she wore it tied neatly in a bun on her head. I sensed this was her first job, for she seemed timid for a barmaid. "Would you like another beer, milady?" she asked Vistilia.

"Yes, please."

Turning to me after filling the mug from a pitcher, she asked, "Are you certain you wouldn't like a drink, milord?"

"I—"

"He doesn't drink . . . this early in the day," Vistilia answered for me, laughing at her choice of words.

"Very well."

"If you are going to be working later this evening, I may stop in for a drink," I told her, unable to look away from her throat.

Being polite and courteous, the barmaid answered, "I will be here, milord. I look forward to your visit."

"And I look forward to your service," I told her, craving not the beer in her pitcher, but the life that pumped beneath her skin.

With a bow, she returned to her duties of cleaning tables, collecting money, and refilling mugs.

I turned away suddenly, taking a deep breath to calm the hunger that I felt growing within me. "So after my drink this evening, what are we to do?" I asked Vistilia.

She leaned back and placed her feet in an adjacent chair. "We have all the time in the world. You tell me."

I thought for a moment, remembering our home

in Crete and the destruction wrought by giants. "Let's head northwest. I want to see the armies of the surrounding kingdoms with my own eyes."

"We can do that," she answered with a smile.

CHAPTER VI

NIGHTMARISH CREATURES

We traveled day and night. We rode side by side. We talked. We laughed. During the day, I wore my cloak to keep the sun from my skin. While the horses rested and drank from lakes and streams, Vistilia watched me drink from rabbits and deer.

We came upon a small village at the foot of the mountains. The town's people took notice but quickly went back to their everyday life of gardening and blacksmithing. They were extremely poor compared to the people of Greece.

We tied our horses at the town tavern and stepped inside. The place was nearly full, but everyone still turned to see the two new faces. We pulled our hoods back, and I found us a small table to sit at while Vistilia made her way to the bar.

The barkeep, a sturdy fella with gray hair tied

back and wearing a dirty apron, greeted her with a friendly smile. "Good afternoon. My name is Bilford, and I'm the owner of this very fine establishment. What is it I can get for ya today?"

"We'll take the bread and brew," Vistilia answered.

"All right," he answered. He poured two steins of beer and placed two loaves of bread in a basket for her.

Vistilia handed him a bit more than it was worth.

"Thank you kindly. If you need anything more, you need only ask."

Vistilia thanked him, and brought the bread and brew to our table.

I tore off a bite of bread and placed it in my mouth. I was sickened by the taste and, trying not to draw attention, spat the bread into my hand. I didn't want be rude and throw it in the floor, so I sat it on the table. "Normal food tastes old now," I told Vistilia, being careful to keep my voice low.

"I'm sorry, sweetheart," Vistilia said sadly, pausing momentarily between bites.

I smelled the beer but quickly turned my nose away. I placed it on the table in front of me to appear normal. I looked out the nearest window. The sky had turned gloomy. "I don't want to stay here very long," I told her. "I would like us to leave before dawn."

"Very well," she agreed and finished her drink. She then swapped her empty stein with my full one.

"I keep thinking about what you said under the apple tree," I admitted. "Can you explain what you meant when you said that you're from elsewhere?"

Wiping the beer from her lips, she answered, "I

suppose I can explain it in a way you can understand."

Before I could voice that it was her fault I was ignorant, she continued.

"Imagine all you believe to exist being contained within a small pond. Now imagine that I watch from the bank until I feel it would be more fun to experience life under the water."

I stared at her in complete confusion.

"Perhaps it's too early to explain it," she said, downing the last of her beer. She sat the stein down, and placed her hand on mine. "Let's go, my love. Let's take a walk through town."

We stood and walked arm in arm toward the door.

Bilford spoke up as we began to leave. "If you need a place to stay for a night or three, I have vacant rooms available."

"Thank you. We will stay," Vistilia answered him. "We are going out for a while but will be back before you close for the night."

Just as I opened the door to step outside the tavern, Bilford added, "Then you should be back before dusk."

We looked back to the barkeep for a reason why he closed so early.

"We have lost many to the fearsome strigoi," he answered our unspoken question, and the bar fell completely silent.

"Strigoi?" I repeated the strange word.

"They have haunted this town since its beginning," Bilford continued. "They come down from the mountain at night to feed on the living, for they are the undead."

"We will be indoors before dark," Vistilia assured him.

We stepped outside and closed the door behind us. Because I was thinking of what the barkeep said about the strigoi, I had forgotten to pull my hood up before stepping out. I then remembered that it was still during the daylight hours, and as I was grabbing my hood, I realized I didn't need it. I held my out hands, but they didn't burn. I looked up at the sky and saw that thick clouds blocked out the sunlight. I began to laugh with happiness. Vistilia and I took our cloaks off and packed them in our satchels. We then walked arm in arm through the town.

The people there weren't very friendly toward us. They stared long enough to remind us that we were outsiders before they went about their business. There were no smiles or laughter. There were no children at play. The town felt all together . . . cold.

We returned to the tavern with our satchels. The place had completely cleared out. Only the barkeep was there now.

Bilford limped over to take our bags. "Let me help you with those," he said.

I thanked him for taking our satchels and saw why he walked with a limp. He had a wooden right leg from the knee down!

He saw that I noticed so began to talk about it. "It's all right. I get around just fine without it," he assured me. He began to slowly lead us upstairs, taking one step at a time. "I wasn't always an old, crippled barkeep," he laughed. "There was a time when I hunted the undead."

"Really?" I asked, amazed.

"Oh yeah!" he exclaimed. "I traveled from town to town, offering my services of putting the dead back in their beds. There was also the occasional dame or two that I put to bed, but of course, they were still alive! HAAHAAHAA!" he joked, reaching the top of the stairs.

After laughing, I asked, "But what happened to your leg?"

The evening sun, shining through windows at each end of the hall, and candles on small tables lit the hallway. He led us into the first room on the left and placed our satchels down at the foot of an old bed before answering my question.

"Years ago, when I came to this town," he began, "I heard stories about a monster that flew down from the mountain at night, but no one had seen where it slept during the day and returned to tell the tale. I took the job to destroy it and left out early one morning to find the creature's lair. Hidden away in the mountains, I came upon an ancient castle. After venturing inside, I found that there was not one monster but many." He paused a moment, remembering that dreadful day. "The bastards took my leg!" he voiced angrily.

"How were you able to escape?" I asked anxiously.

"HA!" he laughed and began tapping on his head. Ol' Bilford outsmarted them. One key characteristic that most all undead creatures share is a distaste for sunlight," he announced, holding up a finger.

"So why does it destroy them?" I asked.

"Oh it doesn't destroy them," Bilford corrected

me. "I said, they have a distaste for it. I think they associate the bright light and warmth of the sun with fire, and so they remain in darkness where they can also pass unseen."

"Interesting," I said, looking at Vistilia, but she bashfully put her head down.

"But there are many different kinds. I suppose it's possible some are actually harmed by sunlight. Anyways, I will be locking up in a few minutes," he informed us. He used a candle from the hall to light one that was on a nightstand next to the door. "I am going to finish cleaning up downstairs before turning in for the night," he told us. "If you need anything, I will be down the hall."

We thanked him, and Bilford left us to tend to his bar, closing the door behind him. I lay back on the bed, putting my hands behind my head.

"It's been a while since we've had a room to ourselves," Vistilia commented, untying her sandals. She then untied mine and tossed them to the floor. She climbed on me and closed the distance between our lips.

I suddenly felt the irresistible urge for blood. "Vistilia, my eternal love, may I drink from you?" I whispered in her ear, my teeth pinching her lobe.

"You may," she breathed. "Drink 'til your heart's content."

I sank my teeth into her neck. Her thoughts were blocked to me, but the blood rushed all the same. She slid a hand under my tunic, and the flickering flame of our candle went out.

We stepped out of the room, and I quietly closed

the door behind us. All the candles had been blown out for the night. Moonlight shined through a window at the end of the hall. We tiptoed down the stairs and through the tavern to the door. We walked outside into the cool night air. There was no one patrolling like in a bigger city. Only the moon lit the village. It was unusually quiet.

Sniffing the air, "There is a foul odor on the wind," I noted aloud.

Vistilia didn't say a word as she followed me to a house across town where my nose led me. I waited a moment outside the door. I listened for any noise coming from within but heard nothing. I tried the door and found it unlocked. Vistilia waited outside as I walked in and made my way quietly through the dark house. As I got closer to the bedroom, I began to hear the sound of something eating. I peaked in to see three pale, slender, winged creatures crouched over a sleeping elderly couple. One was drinking blood from the elderly woman's chest while another was chewing on her thigh! The third creature was feeding on the elderly man's arm. There was also an apparition of an old hag riding the man wildly! The couple was still asleep but seemed to be fighting nightmares.

Disturbed by what I saw, I covered my mouth. The winged creatures must be the strigoi that Bilford warned us about.

The one feeding from the woman's thigh noticed me out of the corner of its eye. It turned and growled. The others then took notice. The apparition shrieked and dissipated. The creature that first noticed me stood tall and flexed its wings to guard their meal. The other two strigoi snatched the elderly couple up from their beds and burst through the ceiling into the night.

I put my hands up and took a step back to show that I didn't wish to fight the creature. The strigoi growled at me again before it flew up through the hole in the ceiling. I breathed deeply and sat down on the floor to regain my composure. I looked up at the night sky through the hole they made in the ceiling. Vistilia sat down and put an arm around me.

"Strigoi are monstrous, nightmarish creatures," I finally said.

Vistilia stood and helped me to my feet. "Come on," she said. "Let's go back to our room."

We walked back to the tavern and quietly slipped into our room. Vistilia blew on the candle and the wick magically burned to life.

I sat on the bed, and deep in thought, I stared off at nothing. Vistilia sat beside me, and I finally spoke. "These attacks must stop. Humans are defenseless against these monsters. Someone must stand up and help them." I turned to look her in the eyes. "I must help them."

I stood and strapped the pilfered short sword to my side. Vistilia picked up our bags. She blew on the candle again, and as you would expect, the flame went out. We walked quietly downstairs. Vistilia left some money on the counter before leaving the tavern. We mounted our horses and rode off in the direction that the strigoi flew.

I led the way up a winding road into the mountains. Through the bare trees, a castle in ruin came into view. Huge wooden doors, which once stood at the castle walls, had long since rotted away. Vistilia and I rode inside and dismounted. Stone pillars and broken blocks from the castle wall were scattered across what used to be a magnificent courtyard. Straight ahead was a large structure with towers connected. I covered my nose and mouth from the foul odor in the air.

"They're here, and they're coming," I warned.

Also sensing the danger, our horses ran out of the courtyard. I didn't try stopping them; they were smart to run. Nervously, I scanned all around, wondering from which direction the creatures would come. I didn't draw my sword immediately; I wanted to communicate with the creatures, if I could. Of course, Vistilia wasn't nervous. She merely stood by, watching as if waiting for a play to begin.

"Sweetheart," she called, "if you're not planning to kill them, what is it that you're going to say?"

Before I could answer, nine strigoi flew from the towers. They circled overhead, diving down to scare us. Then the ghostly old hag that I saw earlier floated out to us, accompanied by a ghostly old man. The circling strigoi landed to block our escape.

"The ghostly woman is a succubus, my love. The man, an incubus," Vistilia whispered. "They're much more dangerous than strigoi."

"We've come peacefully to meet with you," I said to the surrounding creatures, but they did not answer.

We stood our ground as the succubus and incubus smelled of us. Vistilia began to doze off to sleep as the ghostly old man slowly enveloped her in its light. The succubus changed its form to look like Vistilia. It stared deeply into my eyes to put me in a trance and closed its arms around me.

While the succubus held me, I instinctively

began feeding from its ethereal energy and slowly began drifting off to sleep. I threw my arms out to fight the spell. "ENOUGH!" I yelled.

I broke free from my captor, and it was enraged. It reverted to its old hag-like form and gave a terrible shriek.

I checked on Vistilia to find she was still caught up in the incubus' embrace. She was held a few feet above the ground.

"Vistilia! Vistilia!" I yelled, trying to call her out of sleep, but she didn't seem to hear me.

I turned to watch my back and saw one of the strigoi closing in. I unsheathed my sword and split its face open with one quick motion. All the strigoi moved in on me. I held them off as best I could, but the strigoi's wounds didn't seem to slow them down. I fought for several moments before finally killing one! The headless body fell to the ground and crumbled to dust! Fueled by that small victory, I knew now their weakness. I stayed low to the ground, dodging attacks, and I was able to take out four more of the creatures fairly easily.

Through the barrage of attacks from the re-maining strigoi, the succubus flew toward me. I swung my sword, but it passed right through without harming it. The ghostly creature knocked me to the ground, so it seemed to become solid at will. The four strigoi leaped on me, tossed my sword away, and started biting chunks of flesh out of me! I screamed out in agony as I was being eaten alive!

From where I was, I could see Vistilia still caught in the incubus' spell. I exploded with anger and, with a magical force, threw the strigoi away from me! I scrambled to my sword. The strigoi took to the air, flying toward me. As I ran, I reached out to grab my sword. Without knowing the power that I had acquired from the succubus, I willed the sword into my open hand. I quickly turned to strike the approaching strigoi and cut one across the chest. As I fought the four strigoi, my sword began to glow! I sidestepped one of the flying strigoi's attacks and sliced its head off. I blocked another's attack, cutting its arm off and then its head.

Catching a glimpse of movement from the corner of my eye, I turned and thrust my sword. This time, my sword penetrated the succubus, gravely wounding it! It shrieked wickedly in my face and dissipated.

The last two strigoi clawed at me from the air. I ducked beneath and strafed their attacks. I ran across the courtyard, up one of the fallen pillars, and leaped into the air toward one of the approaching strigoi, cleaving it in two.

The last strigoi, the one with the wounded chest, caught me from the side and slammed me hard against the wall of one of the towers. My sword's blade snapped on impact against the stone. The monster dropped me and circled around the courtyard.

I got up from the ground and noticed that, even though my sword was broken, a ghostly light extended the blade to its original length. I dropped the sword, and when it hit the ground, the light quickly went out. The winged beast set its eyes on me and began its approach. I looked at my hand and concentrated on recreating the ghostly sword. An ethereal short sword formed in my hand, and I met the strigoi in combat!

It flew with its claws out, ready to rip me to

pieces. I swung my sword and cut its left wing half in two. The monster shrieked and fell hard to the ground. It stood up and, with a loud grunt, ripped off its half-amputated wing, tossing it to the side.

I took a deep breath and attacked the creature. It caught my wrists and attempted to overpower me. We seemed to be equally matched as we held each other in place. The beast flapped its right wing into the side of my face and kicked me in the chest. I fell to the ground, and my ethereal sword dissipated. The strigoi leaped at me, but I summoned a new ethereal sword and decapitated the monster. The body collapsed on me and crumbled to dust.

I quickly got to my feet and ran to my imprisoned Vistilia. Still suspended in air, I reached up to grab her ankle, but she was immovable within the incubus' grasp. I jumped and was able to hang onto it. Immediately, I began to feel the soothing warmth envelope me and began to fall asleep again. I opened my mouth and sank my teeth into the incubus' neck. I started to feed, and the incubus' ghostly light began to fade as it weakened. Vistilia's eyes opened, and she dropped from the incubus' hold. I continued to feed as it slowly lowered to the ground. I fed on the incubus until it could no longer hold its form and dissipated.

Vistilia locked her fingers behind my neck, and with the bat of her lashes, she said, "My hero."

"Always playing games," I whispered before kissing her. "For someone with unimaginable power, you sure like to make me work," I added, and we both laughed.

"It's the only way for you to grow, and I would never let you get into more trouble than I think you can handle," she answered.

"Speaking of being in trouble, we should find out what became of the elderly couple that were taken from their bed."

"Yes, we should," she agreed, dusting me off.

I took her hand in mine, and we ran into the old castle. Moonlight shined through a large portion of the ceiling that had collapsed, leaving the floor riddled with broken stone. We walked carefully across the large room and found that the king and queen's thrones were also destroyed, possibly during the collapse. Behind the thrones was a large hole in the floor. My night vision cut through the darkness to see that there was a room below us. The room reeked of decay. I listened for a moment but heard nothing, so I dropped down through the hole. Making a quick look around, I motioned to Vistilia that it was safe to follow.

It wasn't much of a room but more of a corridor, and the walls, the walls were constructed of human flesh and bone! Taking hold of her hand, we made our way cautiously down the corridor.

I thought the wind was blowing in behind us, but I soon realized that it was coming from the walls! The walls were breathing! Thinking we should turn back, we saw that the way was shut! The walls had closed us off from making an escape, and skeletal arms extended along the corridor holding torches that suddenly burst into pale green flames to illuminate the way.

"We have no choice but to follow this corridor to its end," I whispered with a bit of fear in my voice. I was afraid. I could feel it growing in the pit of my stomach. I took a deep breath of the foul air to right myself, but it sickened me. I immediately vomited blood onto the floor. Vistillia held me to keep me stable.

A cackling laughter broke out from the walls.

"It would seem your nausea eased the tension of this place, as well as the contents of your belly."

I couldn't help but laugh at my wonderful wife's astute observation. I wiped the blood from my mouth, and we continued slowly down the dark passage.

The living corridor appeared to be shifting to lead us deep down into the mountain. The way behind us continued to close off, but I became more interested in the unknown ahead than what was known behind.

"Where are you leading us?" I finally asked aloud. If the walls could laugh, perhaps they could speak.

"TO TAKE AUDIENCE WITH THE KING, OF COURSE," the corridor echoed. "HE IS MOST INTERESTED IN MEETING YOU." Like the laughter, it was many voices that spoke in unison.

The moldering corridor led us into a throne room where two chairs constructed of bones sat atop a staircase of the dead. The wall divided, and a stitched rug of flesh rolled out. Two corpses floated into the room, hand in hand, over the dreadful carpet; a ghastly sight to behold. With tarnished crowns upon their heads and clothed in tattered robes, no doubt they were once the king and queen of the derelict castle above.

Out of respect, Vistilia and I kneeled before them as they took the throne.

With a cold, raspy voice that sucked air, the king spoke. "Arise."

Standing, I said, "Thank you, Your Maj—"

"SILENCE!" the undead king yelled. "For what purpose are you in my presence, and why have you slain our servants?"

"I witnessed an attack and the abduction of an elderly couple. I followed their abductors to this castle. I came with peaceful intentions but . . ."

He cut me off with a growling bite. "They were commanded to kill anything that enters the castle walls," the king explained, "but no matter, I can create more," he added.

"Where is the elderly couple?" I questioned strongly.

"Our servants needed sustenance. The mortals provided it," the queen answered with the same raspy voice as the king. "Their remains were added to the wall," she added, gesturing toward the mass of flesh and bones that surrounded us.

I glanced over my shoulder and saw that the room was completely sealed off by the wall of mortal remains. I felt fear growing within me again. I didn't like being sealed up like that. My grip tightened on Vistilia's hand.

"Exciting, isn't it?" she whispered to me, her eyes gleaming in the green torchlight.

I needed to distract myself from the growing feeling of dread. "How did you create all this?" I asked the king.

Sitting up regally, he answered, "You don't become king without having power."

"And what is this power you possess?"

"I can raise and control the dead," he answered with a rotten grin.

He stood and floated down to look me over. He was nearly a foot taller than I. Vistilia and I kept still as he circled us.

"You both wear a human guise, but I sense something strangely familiar about you," he said to me. His breath was absolutely atrocious. "What is your name?" he asked.

Suddenly afraid to give him my real name, I quickly decided to give him my father's. "Magnus, your Majesty, and this is my wife." Just by saying his name, I felt a renewed sense of courage begin to break through the fear that had overtaken me within the depths of this decrepit castle of the dead!

He moved in close to smell me, but I didn't flinch. "What sort of creature are you?" he questioned. He then sniffed Vistilia, and I exhaled a breath of anger.

"Answer the question, boy," the queen demanded from atop her throne.

"I don't know what I am."

"Liar!" the queen yelled, standing from her throne.

"Well, Magnus," he began, "I can tell you this: You and your wife inhabit fine bodies." A sly grin crept across his face. "I think I will take them."

Suddenly, many hands grabbed us from behind! The wall had moved close enough to ensnare us. I strained to pull away but couldn't break free!

Vistilia didn't try to escape; she was looking to me to get us out of this mess.

"What are you going to do with our bodies?" I growled.

"My queen and I would like to be beautiful again," he answered, touching Vistilia's face with the back of his dead fingers. "And you are beautiful, so full of life and warmth."

"Well, you can't have us!" I yelled. An ethereal

sword formed in my hand, and with a twist of my wrist, I cut the wall that held me. I was then able to pull away and cut the hands that held Vistilia.

The king drew a dagger and sliced my face! He then floated out of reach of my swing. Licking the blood that he had taken from my cheek, a shiver ran through him. "Your blood tastes . . . unique. I can only imagine how delicious your exquisite wife tastes."

His queen grabbed Vistilia and threw her into the throne. Seeing my anger swell, the king let out a cackling laugh. Surprising him with my speed, I leaped forward and severed his arm. His dagger fell harmlessly to the floor. Before I could take his head, he pushed me back with an invisible force.

"CENTURIONS!" he called out, and the walls began pulling apart to form soldiers.

Vistilia and I ran to each other, meeting in the center of the room as it quickly filled with the king's undead army. They were armed with rusty swords and wore mismatched pieces of rusty armor.

"Are you okay?" I asked Vistilia, looking over her for any wounds.

"I'm fine, dear," she answered. With the growing thunder of soldiers forming around us, we turned to stand back to back. "So, Magnus," she began with a laugh, "how do you plan to get us out of this?"

"I was sort of hoping you would lend a hand," I told her.

"You mean you would share all this fun with little ol' me?" she asked in the sweetest of voices.

Chuckling, I said, "I wouldn't want you to feel left out."

The queen handed her king his severed arm, still

clutching the dagger. While holding his arm to its proper place, strands of muscle reached to reattach it.

With the wall separating, an exit could now be seen, albeit filled with an undead army.

"This may be our best chance, so we need to act," I whispered to Vistilia. "Do I need to hold your hand, or can you keep up?"

"PFF," she blew. "I can handle myself."

"Well, sweetheart," I smiled as a ghostly shield formed in my left hand and a short sword in my right, "let's fight our way out."

Taking heads and arms, I began cutting a path to our escape. The centurion's ancient blades were no match for my ethereal one, so I was able to take them down easily. The tricky part was keeping them down. Because they were animated corpses, they just kept coming, reattaching their severed limbs or even their head!

That's where Vistilia surprised me. As I was decapitating and shield bashing our way through a sea of undead soldiers, my lovely Vistilia turned them to dust with merely a touch. With an open palm, she pushed them into oblivion.

Up the long tunnel we fought, slashing, smashing, and disintegrating. Far behind us, I could still hear the king yelling. The centurions began fusing together again to block our escape. I released my sword, took hold of Vistilia's hand, and charged through the thin wall of undead with my shield. The tunnel ahead of us was clear, so we ran quickly toward the exit.

Jumping up through the broken floor of the castle, we breathed in deep the fresh, morning air.

"How about we get out of this foul place?" I

asked.

"Yes," she answered. "Let's get out of here. This place is a bit too touchy-feely for me."

From below us, I could hear the soldiers approaching, so I pushed the large, castle stones into the hole to seal them in.

Having left my cloak in a pack on my horse, I waited in the shadows while Vistilia whistled for them to return. Luckily they hadn't wandered far. We mounted up and continued our way northwest over the mountains.

CHAPTER VII

DARK DAUGHTER

After weeks of traversing rugged mountains, we were glad to reach one of our neighboring kingdoms, but it seemed the farther north we traveled from the Mediterranean, the smaller the human settlements became.

I slipped quietly into the torch lit castle of this kingdom's ruler, and crept from shadow to shadow to elude the patrolling guards. I located the king's bed chamber, and he confided in me while he slept. His blood drowned my thirst and revealed to me what I had come fearing: Their soldiers were indeed few in number and ill-equipped for battling giants, but then I could've seen that without drinking from his memories. The soldiers of the many villages he ruled over were nothing more than experienced hunters given leather armor painted with the king's insignia.

By sunrise, Vistilia and I were sitting at the town's eatery. It was just a few long tables under a roof, but at least it and the surrounding trees kept the sun off me. Vistilia was enjoying a healthy looking breakfast of bacon, eggs, and potatoes.

"You miss it?" she asked me as she crunched on her bacon.

"What, breakfast? I miss sharing a meal with you, yes."

She reached across the table to rub my face before leaning in for a kiss.

We sat quietly for a moment while she ate her breakfast. I breathed in the cool, morning air and watched as children came outside to play. Seeing them run off together caused me to smile and remember my childhood years.

Vistilia and I would stash acorns for a week before our annual Acorn War with the other children of Atronos. We may have helped each other gather acorns to be used as ammunition, but when the war began, no one took sides. It was every kid for themselves! It was so much fun, and we all looked forward to it every year.

"Talk to me, sweetheart," Vistilia said, taking a bite of potatoes. "Tell me what's on your mind."

I placed my hand on hers before speaking. "We weren't able to have children in life, but what if we made one now?"

She tilted her head, and a smile formed from her lips. "Like you?" she asked. "A vampire?"

"A what?"

"Like the king, his queen, and their army, you are undead," she began to explain. "In other words, you have beaten death by returning from the grave. You can still be killed, but neither age nor disease holds any power over you. There are many types of undead, just as there are many types of vampires in the world. I combined characteristics of different kinds of vampires to make you unique. You already know that you need blood to survive, and through blood, you can see the thoughts and memories of your victims. You have also learned that you can gain new abilities this way. When you drank from the succubus, you gained the ability to conjure and manipulate ethereal energy."

Suddenly, it dawned on me. "So, by drinking blood, I can take power. By giving blood, I may bestow it."

Vistilia nodded in agreement.

"My love," I began, taking both her hands in mine before asking, "would you prefer a son or a daughter?"

With a smile, she answered, "How about both?"

At that very moment, a man ran out into the center of the village. "Our king has been attacked!" he shouted out to everyone. "He is alive but very weak. A sacrifice must be made to appease the gods. A life must be taken to protect us and our king from this evil."

The frightened townspeople began gathering their children and locking up their homes. Even the cook doused out his fire and carried his pots and utensils indoors.

A robed man walked out, stood next to the announcer, and unrolled a scroll. After looking over it for a moment, he pointed to a house. The king's announcer knocked forcefully on the door until it was opened by the man of the house. The man had tears in his eyes as he led his crying daughter outside. The man's wife begged them not to take their little girl. When the girl was handed over, the man held his wife while she screamed and clambered to save their daughter.

"They're not going to kill that little girl because I drank from their king, are they?" I asked Vistilia in disbelief.

"It would appear so," she answered without turning away from the spectacle.

With tears in his eyes, the girl's father pulled his screaming wife indoors.

Shaded from the morning sun, I watched as more men came to assist in the ritual. A fire pit was lit while the robed man recited a prayer to their gods for the village's protection. Cries from the girl's mother could still be heard from within their home. Three men took hold of the little girl. One stood behind to hold the girl still as the other two held her arms out to the robed man.

I can't let this innocent child be killed, but I don't know if I can save her, I thought to myself. There's quite a distance of sunlight between us.

"What are you going to do?" Vistilia asked me.

"Can't you save her?" I asked frantically with the rising sound of prayer, a mother's screams, and the crackling fire!

"It is your decision to make. Will you act or will you watch?"

The robed man pulled a long, sharpened stone from his belt and slashed the child's wrists! The girl screamed out in pain! Ignoring the burning rays of the sun, I ran to save her! I ran faster than I imagined possible. I saw the men begin to toss the bleeding girl into the fire pit when I stepped in and swept her up in my arms! I ran through the village toward the shade of the forest. I could smell my hair and skin burning away as I weakened in the morning light. I reached the tree line and collapsed with the girl in my arms.

If I was going to save this little girl, I needed to act fast! I may have saved her from the fire, but she will bleed to death soon. I could barely see through my clouded eyes, but I could hear the girl's beating heart fighting to stay alive!

Wiping the hair from her face, I whispered, "Listen to me, sweet girl. You must drink to stay alive. You must. Do you understand?"

Her eyes shuddered but were too weak to open, so she nodded that she understood.

When I started to open a vein for her, I gasped at the sight of my arms. My skin had burned to ash in the morning sun! I peeled the flesh back with my fingers and pressed my arm to the child's mouth for her to drink.

Vistilia reached the shade of the forest and watched as I gave my blood to save this little girl from death.

Seeing her wrists still oozing blood, I took one for a taste. I was happy to feel her heart growing stronger! I pulled my teeth away and saw that my blood wasn't healing her quick enough.

"Will it take eight days for her to change, like it did me?" I asked Vistilia.

"No. It won't take nearly that long."

"But how do I stop her wounds from bleeding?"

"Try putting some of your blood directly on her wrists," she suggested.

As the girl continued drinking from my right arm, I bit a finger on my left hand and rubbed my blood into her wounds. Within seconds, I could see her flesh close the wounds shut! I licked the remaining blood from her arms as she slowed her drinking from mine.

"The beast is feeding on her!" I heard one of the villagers yell. I turned to see four men running toward the forest carrying spears!

I stood to lead the girl and Vistilia deeper into the forest but staggered with dizziness from giving so much blood and being burned by the sun!

A spear pierced my side! I pulled it out just as the four men entered the forest. The men were horrified by the sight of me. I was able to stand while they approached cautiously. I stood between them and the girl lying on the ground behind me. I held the spear to keep the men away, and they kept their spears set on me to keep me away. The man that had thrown his spear kept a bit more distance, staying behind his comrades.

The soldier on my left, hit my spear with his, knocking the point toward the ground, while the two other spearmen lunged. The two spears entered my abdomen, and I yelled out in pain! Channeling that pain, I hit all four of the men with an invisible force that sent them flying away from me. I fell to my knees and pulled a spear from my stomach. I threw it, pinning one man to a tree. I removed the other spear, but the three remaining men ran out of the forest.

I took a deep breath and rubbed my head. My hair had completely burned away. I delicately felt of my face to find that my nose and lips were gone! I crawled to the man that I had speared to the tree. His blood soothed my pain and began healing my extensive injuries.

After drinking all that I could from him, I turned my attention back to the young girl. She wasn't moving!

I hurried to her and lifted her head from the ground. She wasn't breathing! "Vistilia!" I cried out.

"Yes, beloved," she answered.

I turned to find her sitting in a tree. She had been watching me fight off the spearmen from that lofty perch.

"She has died! We have lost her." I pulled the girl close and held her in my arms. Tears streamed down my face. I wiped them away to find they were tears of blood, and I had stained my hand.

Vistilia dropped down from her tree and sat next to me, putting her arm around me.

Like an earthquake far beneath the ocean, I heard it! A heartbeat! Seconds later, I heard it beat again. Slowly, I heard her heart build a rhythm, and the blood she drank from me began coursing through her veins.

"You saved her," Vistilia said, laying her head against my shoulder. "You saved our little girl. I'd kiss you, if you had lips," she laughed. "You look terrible, sweetheart, but you'll be okay," she assured me. "Your wounds will heal."

I gently placed the girl in the leaves of the forest floor. Vistilia wiped her dirty face. Her hand instantly removed the soot and grime that covered her. She ran her fingers through the girl's tangled mess of hair, and it instantly smoothed. She felt the fabric of her plain dress, and it changed to a pretty, new dress. She touched the tops of her bare feet, and sandals magically formed around them.

I had so many questions for her, but we didn't have time for that now; I could hear the people gathering in the village. "We should get moving," I told her. "I'm in no shape to fight off more soldiers, and I'm sure the king will send more soon."

"You're right. We do," she agreed. "If you lead the way, I'll carry her."

"What about the horses?"

"It's best to leave them behind. I'm sorry." She picked up the still sleeping girl and followed me deep into the forest.

We hiked for hours until we reached the bank of a river. We couldn't travel any further until the afternoon sun set, so we rested.

Vistilia sat the girl down, and she opened her eyes! Frightened by the sight of me, she huddled up close to Vistilia.

"It's okay, sweetie," my dear wife assured her. "He got hurt while saving you. He'll be okay soon, so don't worry yourself."

The girl turned her head to look at me. "You will get better?" she asked in a low voice.

"Yes. I just need to rest a little while," I answered her, sitting with my back against a tree. "I'm glad you're feeling better," I told her. "What's your name?"

"Evelyn," she answered sweetly.

"That sure is a pretty name, Evelyn; a pretty name for a pretty girl."

She blushed. "Yeah."

Vistilia smiled at me. "Can you tell him how old you are?" she whispered in her ear.

"Eleven."

"Evelyn's eleven," Vistilia said. "How precious!"

My eyes connected with Vistilia's as if we were

sharing the same thought: We are a family now. I thought again how this life was unfolding differently from the previous one. I am not the Manius that I once was, but my father's strength and my mother's cunning will never leave me. The dark blood that flows through me now flows through this little girl . . . our little girl. "My name is Magnus," I told my daughter.

She was a little ray of sunshine in the shadow of the forest. Standing barefoot at 4'8" tall, she had long, blonde hair and crystal blue eyes.

Vistilia placed a hand lightly on her back and asked, "Will you give him a hug? It would make him feel better."

She seemed to shy away a bit but slowly came towards me. I was still sitting down with my back against the tree, so I leaned forward for her to put her arms around me. It did make me feel better. "Thank you."

She sat down next to me, so Vistilia came over to sit next to her in the leaves while we waited for sunset. The three of us sat together with our backs against the large tree.

"I'm getting hungry," Evelyn told us.

Vistilia glanced at me, and I took a deep, regretful breath because I was going to have to teach this innocent, little girl how to survive as a vampire.

Darkness came before we stepped out of the forest. Vistilia sat on a rock at the water's edge while I stood with Evelyn on the moonlit riverbank. I explained to her that the sun had disfigured me when I rushed to save her, and it would do the same to her now. "You must stay shielded from the sun," I told her.

"Why did my father let those men hurt me?" she

asked, her question catching me off guard.

I held her hand in mine and got down on one knee to look her straight in the eyes, taking a moment to think how to explain it to a child. "Sunshine, your parents loved you dearly, but they couldn't keep you. They had to give you away. Those men who hurt you were going to send you to their gods, but I didn't want them to."

"So you saved me?"

"Yes, I saved you. We are your parents now, Vistilia and I, and we will take care of you."

She hugged me, and then ran to Vistilia to hug her. Vistilia stood from the rock, where she was sitting with her bare feet in the river, to catch Evelyn in her arms. Laughing, Vistilia spun her around before kissing her cheek and putting her down.

Past them, farther down the riverbank, I spotted a herd of deer gathering for a drink of water. I motioned to Vistilia to quiet down, and she turned to see what I was focused on. I made my way over to them and pointed for Evelyn to look. She was excited when she saw the herd.

I whispered in her ear, "Do you think you can catch one?"

She looked at me with an astonished expression. I took her hand and led her quickly along the tree line. She was amazed by her newly gifted speed, and we were soon standing among the herd without their notice. I grabbed the antlers of a grown buck and, with a sharp twist, broke his neck. The rest of the deer finally took notice of us and quickly ran back into the forest.

"Would you like me to collect some firewood?" my little girl asked, ready for dinner.

"We don't need it," I told her. "We can only drink from it."

Her excitement was replaced with confusion, so I took the first drink. I bit into the deer's neck and let its life flow into me. "Fresh blood is what keeps you alive now," I explained.

She hesitantly touched her tongue to the blood oozing over the deer's bristly hair. Her lips quivered from the taste. She touched her teeth to find two of them had grown longer. She then made her own bite on the deer's neck, so we drank together until we could drink no more.

"You're looking better," Vistilia stated, walking up next to us.

"I'm feeling better," I confirmed. Examining my arms, they did appear to be healing. I lightly touched my face to find it too was quickly returning to normal.

"Can we go home now?" Evelyn asked us.

My wife and I glanced at one another before I told our daughter, "We don't have a home, but we will. We'll find us a home."

Evelyn became excited and hugged me.

"So how are we crossing this river?" Vistilia asked.

Thinking for a moment, I answered, "We may have to swim it."

"But I don't know how to swim," Evelyn admitted.

"Then I'll carry you across." I bent down for her to climb onto my back.

"I'll see you on the other side, dear," I told Vistilia, giving her a kiss before I stepped into the water.

"I'm scared," Evelyn whispered into my ear,

tightening her arms around me.

For a moment, I caught a glimpse of her thoughts. Her fear of drowning was so strong that I could feel it! I gasped but quickly returned my focus to getting her across safely. "We'll be all right," I tried to assure her. "Just hold on tight. We'll be on the other side soon."

The river's current wasn't too strong, so we weren't pulled downstream far before reaching the rocky shore.

Evelyn saw that Vistilia was already there, waiting for us. "How'd she get over here so quickly?" she asked, amazed.

"Why don't you ask her; she won't tell me."

She dropped down from my back and ran to her.

"You did great, sweetie," Vistilia said, giving her a hug.

"How did you get over here? You're not even wet!" Evelyn said, feeling of Vistilia's dress.

"And neither are you," she answered with a smile."

Evelyn looked down at her dress and saw that she was completely dry! "How did you do that?"

"I can do whatever I want."

"Well, didn't you want us to make it across the river just as easily as you?" I asked bitterly, taking Evelyn's hand and continuing on into the forest.

"Sweetheart," she said, following us, "don't be like that. All this is just for fun."

I quickly turned to face her. "Fun? You think this is some sort of game?"

"Yes," she answered. "For me, it is just a game," she clarified.

Shaking my head, I told her, "This isn't a game for us."

Evelyn stood next to me, squeezing my hand tighter as our voices grew louder.

"You're playing with people's lives here!" I argued. "Do you think it was fun for me to take those spears into my stomach? Do you think it was fun for me to be disfigured by something as simple as sunlight? This little girl's own parents gave her up to be sacrificed to their god while a god was right there letting it happen!"

Tears welled up in her eyes before she spoke. "I'm sorry. You're right. It may be just a game to me, but I forget that this is all you know."

"You're not going to fight anymore, are you?" Evelyn asked us. She too had tears in her eyes, but they were tears of blood.

It broke my heart to see her cry, to see them both cry. "I'm sorry," I told them. I took Vistilia's hand and pulled her to me. The three of us held each other there in the dark forest.

With her arms still around me, Vistilia said, "I believe it would be best if I left."

I pulled away from her, not believing what she just said. "What? What do you mean?"

She turned to look toward the river that we had just crossed. "I see now that my abilities are creating a rift between us. Knowing that I can alter reality with a simple thought, you focus more on why I don't make life perfect for you instead of working to overcome obstacles on your own." Facing me, she could see the heartbreak in my eyes. "I fear, if I stay, you will grow to hate me, and I don't want that. I don't want that," she emphasized with tears in her eyes.

"But we've always been together," I finally said, shocked by her decision. "I can't live without you. I don't want to live without you. I may disagree with how you use your powers, but I could never hate you. I love you. I love you with every fiber of my being. I don't want you to go. Don't you love me anymore?" With that, crimson tears broke from my eyes and streamed down my face.

"Oh, Manius, I do love you," she said, holding me again. "I love you dearly."

"Where are you going?" Evelyn asked innocently.

Vistilia got down on her knees to be eye level with her. "Well, sweetie, I live in a world a lot like this one, only far in the future."

"I don't understand," Evelyn admitted.

"So you traveled through time?" I asked her.

"I can in this world, but that's not how I got here," she answered. She thought for a moment how to explain. "The wizards of my world made it so everyone can have their own space to live in and control," she said, holding her arms out to everything around us.

"You and your people are gods indeed, if you created everything," I told her.

"We may seem like gods here, but in my world, we are just normal people."

"But how can normal people create an entire world and all its inhabitants?" A more pressing question dawned on me, and I suddenly felt my blood begin to boil. "It was you. You did this. You created the giants! You allowed them to destroy our home," I said in disbelief. I pointed a sharp finger at her. "You could have stopped it! You could have saved everyone!"

"I told you, you would hate me," she said, her lips quivering as she fought back her tears.

"How could you?" I yelled. "My family took you in. They took care of you! They loved you like their own daughter. You have all this power, and yet you allow so much death and suffering. I thought you had made me into a monster, but you are the real monster here, aren't you?"

"I'm leaving, Manius," she told me, sniffling and wiping her eyes. "I'm going home, to my home."

I took a deep breath to try and relax. I stood calmly, listening to her every word, but I was seething beneath the surface. She's played me for a fool my entire life! She's taken everything from me!

"You won't see me, but I'll be able to see and hear you. When the weight of the world becomes too much to bear, I'll return. Remember: A millennium to you is but a moment to me."

"I thought I meant more to you than this, Vistilia. I thought you loved me," I expressed coldly.

"I know you don't fully understand it now, but maybe one day you will and think better of me. Goodbye, my darling husband. I will always love you." She kissed my callous lips tenderly, and in a bright flash of light, she was gone.

My wife, my love, my lifelong friend was gone. I felt as if a hole suddenly opened within me, and I trembled from the pain she had wrought. My legs could no longer support me, and I fell to my knees and sobbed. For the first time in all my life, I was alone.

It was then I realized that Evelyn was gone too! I turned to look in every direction, but even with my sharp, unnatural vision, she was nowhere in sight. "Evelyn!" I called. "Please come back! EVELYN! EVE!"

I ,searched the ground where I last saw her standing. I found a disturbance left in the fallen leaves leading away from me. I ran, following the subtle path deep into the forest.

I soon spotted her sitting on a creek bank with her knees pulled up tight against herself. I walked up slowly and sat next to her. Her face was wet with the red tears that she had cried, so I helped wash her face.

She leaned her head against my shoulder, and we sat together in silence for hours, listening to the soft flowing water of the stream.

CHAPTER VIII

DARK SON

Dawn came, and beams of sunlight broke through the trees.

"It burns!" Evelyn cried to me, cowering from the burning rays.

"We're okay," I calmed her. "The forest is thick enough to protect us."

We sat in the shade of the trees for half the day. Dark clouds blew in thunder showers just after noon. Taking advantage of the overcast, we hiked through the pouring rain and wet forest until we found a well-worn path.

"Magnus, I'm hungry," she told me, taking hold of my hand.

"I know you are, Eve. I am too. We'll find something soon."

We followed the muddy road for a little more

than an hour before coming upon a quaint, little town. I looked over my hands and arms to make sure they had healed enough to not draw attention. They looked fine but hairless. I rubbed my face and head to find they were the same.

"Now, Eve," I began, laying out a few rules for her, "it would be best if you said nothing about me saving you from the fire. Don't tell anyone that Vistilia disappeared in a big flash of light, and you shouldn't mention that you drink blood either. Do you understand?"

"What about you catching that deer?" she asked with an excited look on her face.

I shook my head, which killed her excitement.

"What about the sun burning us?"

I shook my head again. "Nothing about that either."

"Are we supposed to know each other?" she asked, discouraged that she couldn't tell anyone about the adventure she was now living.

"Just don't tell anyone about the past two days," I chuckled.

"But I didn't know you two days ago."

"Evelyn!" I scolded, laughing at her.

"Okay. Okay," she finally agreed.

Soaking wet, we walked through the town looking for shelter from the rain when a brewery seemed like the perfect place for a drink! We walked inside with a sigh of relief to be indoors from the downpour. The place was lit by a large fireplace and candles on five tables, but there were no customers. I supposed they were all home with their families during the storm.

We had entered from a door on the left side of

the brewery. Along the front of the building was a row of windows, and on the far side of the room was a door leading into a house. The fireplace was built in the middle of that far wall and open to both the barroom and the conjoined house.

A fair woman walked in from a door behind the bar. "Oh, just look at you two," she said, grabbing a couple towels before coming around to greet us. "You're positively soaked to the bone."

KA-RACK! Thunder struck so loudly that it rang our ears! Both, the woman and Eve screamed and covered their ears from the sound. I put a hand on Eve's shoulder to comfort her.

The woman handed me a towel, and an expression of shock befell her! "My goodness, what happened to your ears?"

AH, HADES! I forgot to check my ears! I reached up and felt for them. They were there, partially. They felt like a lip of flesh around a hole in my head. "Oh, I was burned," I told her and left it at that.

"I'm sorry to hear that," she said before realizing the rudeness of her apology. "I'm sorry. Is your hearing okay?"

"My hearing is fine, milady. It looks worse than what it truly is."

"It's good you still have your hearing," she said while drying Eve's hair and face. "My name is Adabelle. People 'round here call me Bell," she told us.

"My name's Magnus, and this is my daughter, Evelyn."

Eve turned her head and smiled at me. She liked that I called her my daughter. Turning back to Bell, she said, "People round here call me Eve."

"Well, aren't you just a charming little lady," Bell commented. Turning to me, "Are you from round here? I don't recall seeing either of you before."

"No, milady, we're merely traveling north in search of a new life," I explained.

She pressed her cheek next to Eve's for a moment. "Come near the fire, dear, so you may warm yourself," she said, leading Eve across the barroom. "You've been out in the rain far too long; you're dreadfully cold."

A stout man walked in through the same door that Bell had. "Get wet, did we?" he asked me with a chuckle. "Well, dry off and stick around until the storm passes. We have plenty to drink."

"Thank you, sir. We will," I told him with a chuckle of my own.

"I'll be in back if you need anything. The name's Roland." He filled a large cup with beer from an oak barrel before heading back to his work.

Adabelle pulled a couple chairs over for us to sit next to the fire. "So where is the misses, might I ask?"

"She's . . . gone," I answered sadly, untying my sandals to dry off my feet and legs with the towel she handed me.

"Oh dear, I'm sorry." She touched my shoulder briefly to show her apologies.

She then untied Eve's sandals and began drying off her feet. Eve leaned forward and breathed in deeply the woman's scent while she wasn't paying attention! I pulled her face to me and shook my head.

Bell felt how cold Eve's feet were, even while sitting in front of the fire. "How 'bout I prepare you both a hot bath? I don't want you to take the fever. I can hang your clothes by the fire, and they should be dry by the time you're done."

"That would be very kind of you," I told her. "Thank you for your generosity."

Bell grabbed a thick cloth from the mantle and took a kettle from the fireplace. "We have another fireplace in the back room. It won't take long to get two baths ready. Just rest here for a moment."

Once the woman left the room, I whispered, "Eve, we can't kill humans like we did the deer by the river."

"But I'm hungry," she told me, holding her stomach. "It hurts."

"I know it hurts, but we must be patient. I don't want you to be hurt like I was."

She reached out with her delicate little hand and took hold of mine while we sat by the fire. "I wish Vistilia was here," she told me in a low tone.

Not knowing what to say, I said nothing.

"Did she make us like this?" she whispered.

"Yes," I answered. "She made us. Don't worry yourself though; she'll come back to us when she's ready."

Adabelle peeked into the room and motioned for us to follow her. She led us into the adjacent house and down a hallway towards the back. At the end of the hall was a room with many towels draped over lines to dry. Two wooden tubs were filled with steaming hot water. Lines of towels divided the two tubs to give us a bit of privacy from each other.

"I'll give you a moment to get into your baths," Adabelle told us. "Now, mind you, it's hot," she warned. "Toss your clothes into a pile, and I'll come get them. They should be pretty well dry by the time you're done."

Bell stepped out of the room, so Evelyn and I stripped off our wet clothing behind our curtain of towels and eased into our baths. It felt good to warm my cold skin in the hot bath. Cupping my hands into the water, I washed my face.

Bell heard that we were in our baths, so she stepped in to gather up our clothes. She then carried them down the hall and into the brewery.

Eve slid one of the towels over that divided us. "Now be sure to wash behind your ears," she ordered with a laugh, reminding me that I had no ears to wash behind.

"I think you need to wash behind yours," I joked, throwing water at her between the towels.

She turned her face away, laughing and splashing water at me. "Stop! Stop! Stop!" she laughed.

We stopped splashing water at each other, and I held out my hand to her. She took hold of it, and we relaxed for a few minutes in our warm baths.

"We should finish up, so we can get something to drink," I told her.

"Okay," she agreed. "I'm starving."

I then pulled the towel that she had moved back in its place, so we had privacy as we bathed.

Getting out of the tub, I dried off with one of the hanging towels and wrapped it around my waist. I stood in the doorway with my back to Eve until she dried off. With a towel wrapped around her, she followed me down the hall and into the empty seating area of the brewery where we found our clothes draped over chairs in front of the fireplace. I felt of them, but they weren't quite dry yet.

Adabelle walked in from the back where her husband was working. She had a cutting board with a loaf of bread on it in one hand and a small kettle of soup in the other. "Help yourself to this soup and bread. It's fresh off the fire," she told us as she sat the food on the bar. She then filled a mug with beer and placed it next to the food before walking around to us at the fireplace. Reaching into her apron, she revealed a hairbrush. Eve turned to let her brush her hair.

"Magnus, I poured that pint for you," she told me while brushing Eve's hair with her back to me. "I also have milk for Eve."

"Thank you for the drink, Bell. Thank you for everything. You are too kind."

I reached around quickly to cover her mouth and held her arms while I sank my fangs into her neck. I eased her to the floor and tried pushing my thoughts on her like the succubus did me. "*Shhh. Rest your eyes. Relax. Your body is heavy. Breathe deeply. Drift off to sleep.*"

I felt her body go limp. It worked! I released my bite so Eve could take a drink.

"Is she dead?" Eve asked, worried for the nice lady.

"No, she's just taking a little nap."

"How did you get her to sleep?" Eve whispered.

"I will teach you later. For now, we must be cautious. Drink only a little. We don't want to kill her."

"I won't drink much; I like her," Eve told me before drinking from the bite I made.

I pushed the wet hair from her face before leaving to try the spell on Roland. I walked behind the bar and looked into the back room to see him making wooden barrels. I ran in quickly and grabbed him like I did his wife, putting him to sleep just as easily. I drank slowly, listening to the rhythmic pounding of his heart pump delicious, intoxicated blood to me. It saturated my cold heart and quenched my withering veins.

I heard the door to the bar open and Eve yell for me. "MAGNUS!"

I dropped Roland and dashed into the barroom to find a man holding a knife at my little girl. Reaching out, I clutched the man's weapon with an invisible hand and tore it away from him.

"What devilry is this?" the man yelled, grabbing a chair to use as a shield.

Eve backed away from Adabelle as the man moved closer, holding the chair between them. He stooped to check the woman's condition.

"You needn't worry; Bell is still alive," I told him, making my way slowly around the bar to put myself between him and my daughter. With my heightened senses, I could see the warmth of Bell's blood still pulsing within her.

"Why did this child feel compelled to drink the blood of this woman?" the man asked. "How were you able to take my dagger away from across the room?"

His curiosity outweighed his fear of us, and that interested me. He was a little shorter than I, standing nearly 6'. He had dark hair and brooding eyes.

Keeping an eye on the man, I took Eve's clothing from the chair and handed them to her. "They're dry enough to put on," I told her. "Just step there in the hall and get dressed."

Nervously, she did as I said.

"What's your name, son?"

Still holding the chair like a shield, he answered, "My name is Dirkonus."

"I'm Magnus, and that was my daughter, Eve. Do you mind if I get some clothes on?" I asked, still holding the towel around my waist.

He took a moment to think before taking a step back to allow me to grab my clothes. I stepped behind the bar to get dressed.

I saw Eve look into the room. "Everything's all right," I assured her. "Will you go into the back and heal the wound on Roland's neck?" Before she could ask how, I explained, "Just rub a small amount of your blood on it."

She quickly ran back there to do as I asked. I walked over toward Adabelle, still lying on the floor in front of the fireplace. Dirkonus stepped forward with the chair to block me from her.

"What do you intend to do?" he asked.

"To heal her," I answered nonchalantly.

He watched as I carefully picked her up and sat her at a table. I moved her hair to reveal the bite that I had made earlier. I bit my tongue, wiped the blood from it, and rubbed it into the two punctures on her neck. Dirkonus was astonished to see the wound heal instantly. I then cleaned the excess blood with the towel that I had been wearing and took a seat at another table.

"If you'll sit in that chair instead of imagining it's a shield, I'll answer some of the questions you have," I told him.

Without taking his eyes off me, he sat down at my table.

I reached out toward the mug of beer that Bell

had poured for me, and it came to me. I sat it on the table and magically slid it over for Dirkonus to drink. "You look like you could use a drink," I laughed. "Would you like some bread?" I then brought the cutting board with bread on it the same way as I did the mug of beer. "Bell just took this out of the oven," I told him. "She's a sweet lady."

"Very sweet," Eve added, entering the room, but Dirkonus didn't pick up on our dark humor. She grabbed a couple pieces of wood from a small stack next to the fireplace and tossed them into the fire to keep it burning. She stood in front of it and continued to brush her hair.

The young man turned his mug up for a couple swallows of beer.

"So, Dirkonus, what brought you to this town?"

"Giants," he answered bitterly. "Giants killed my family two springs ago."

"So their tyranny spreads," I thought aloud.

"You've dealt with them too, I take it?"

"More like fled from them," I answered him honestly. "What happened?"

"There were three families of us," he began. "We were traveling south to a port city my father spoke of where people brought goods from all over. We were still days from the city when our camp was attacked," he trailed off, becoming lost in his memories.

"How did you escape?" I asked, bringing him back to the present.

"The brutes came for food. They came for us," he told me, his eyes looking right into mine.

"I know this pain you feel."

"They took my wife!" he cried. "They took my

son!" Tears streamed down his face. "They took my boy!" He sprung from his chair, throwing the mug of beer across the room.

The breaking of the mug woke Adabelle from her nap. "Oh, I'm sorry," she apologized, looking around in confusion. "I must have dozed off."

"Sorry I startled you, Bell," he said, wiping the tears from his face. "I was just recounting my tale."

"And what a dreadful tale it is," Bell added, standing up to go look out the window at the rain beginning to slack off. "There are no giants in these parts, thank the gods. The only trouble that stirs round here comes from those blasted elves."

"Elves?" I questioned. "I've never heard of such creature."

"Then be thankful," she said, turning to face me. "They're not the lumbering monsters of Dirkonus' tale, but a clever lot, they are. They dwell in the hills west of here. Our hunters dare not venture too closely to the hills, for that is the elves' hunting grounds. It is said that their arrows are magical, and they can kill a whole herd of deer with one shot."

"We could use one of those," Eve spoke up, giving Adabelle her brush.

"You are the prettiest little girl," Bell commented, feeling Eve's blonde hair. "I can't believe I fell asleep like I did. I don't even remember sitting down."

"You were tired from all the trouble we put you through," I explained to cover up what really happened.

"Oh, it was no trouble at all."

Dirkonus stepped in saying, "He helped you to a chair where you rested a moment." He then walked over to pick up the broken pieces of the beer mug that he had thrown.

"Don't you worry 'bout that," Bell told him, grabbing a broom from next to the fireplace, but Dirkonus picked up all the pieces that he saw of the mug.

Putting the broken pieces and some money in her hand, he apologized.

She thanked him and asked Eve to bring her the towel that was hanging over a chair. While using the towel to soak up the spilled beer, she noticed blood on it. "Whose towel was this?" she asked.

"That must've been my towel," I admitted.

"Are you okay? Are you hurt?"

"I'm fine," I answered.

She looked at Eve, and I caught a hint of suspicion within her.

"Come with me to get some clean towels," she told Eve, putting an arm around her. "We can't clean up beer with a bloody towel now, can we?"

"The rain has ceased," I said, standing from my chair. "I believe it's time for us to be heading on. Thank you for your kindness."

"Where will you go?" she asked. "It will be dark soon."

I took Eve's hand and began to leave. "Don't worry yourself. We'll be okay."

"Well, if you must go, take this bread with you; you may want it later." Adabelle gave the loaf of bread to Eve and kissed her goodbye on the head.

"I would like to speak with you a bit more," Dirkonus said to me.

I nodded, and we followed Dirkonus outside and across town to his home. The place wasn't as nice as

Roland's and Adabelle's. It was just a small hut built around a fire pit. There was a bed of animal skins opposite from the entrance and a skin keeping the wind out. His only possession was a short spear propped up against the wall.

He took a few pieces of wood that he had stacked away and some kindling to start a fire in his fire pit.

"You never told me how you escaped the giants," I reminded him.

He got the fire started and picked up his spear. It was a simple weapon with a strong oak shaft tipped with a bronze head. He sat down on his furs, starring at the spear.

I motioned to Eve that it was okay for her to sit. She sat, but she sat near the entrance. I took a seat next to the fire.

"This belonged to my father," he began to tell. "He gave it to my older brother before he died that winter. After the coldest months, we decided to move south to the port city, hoping for an easier life."

He paused for a moment to wipe away the tears that were building in his eyes. With a heavy sigh, he continued his story.

"Giants attacked our camp at dawn. My brother and I fought them, but we were outnumbered. They bludgeoned our horses and herded our family. My spear was snapped during the battle, and my brother fell protecting me. I took up the spear that our father passed down to him and fought as if the gods strengthened me. I was able to kill two of the monsters before I fell into the river and was swept away by the current. Broken and alone, I abandoned the move to the port and settled here."

Astonished, I asked, "You were able to kill two giants?"

"I impaled the first one through the neck. I speared the second under the ribs, but when he fell, he took me with him into the river. This spear is all I have left."

"Well, Dirkonus, I believe we can help each other."

"Are you going to teach me that trick how to move things as you do?"

"Oh, there's so much more to it than that," I smiled, clinching my fingers into a fist and forming an ethereal spear. Ghostly smoke swirled slowly along the entire length of the summoned weapon.

"By the gods!" Dirkonus voiced. "I thought humans were incapable of magic."

"I didn't know you could do that," Eve said to me, also surprised.

"By becoming a vampire, knowledge of the arcane is now attainable," I explained.

"What is a vampire?" he asked. "How do you become one?"

I let my spear dissipate while I thought how to explain what I was. "To become a vampire, you must drink the blood of a vampire. Your body will die, but the blood will bring you back."

Turning to Eve, I asked, "Do you still have the bread that Bell gave you?"

She nodded and took it from a pocket in her dress.

"Take a bite of it," I told her.

As soon as she bit, she spat it out and looked at

me in disgust. "Ugh, nasty!"

"What did it taste like?" I asked.

"It tastes like . . . dirt."

"That's because your body is different now," I explained. "A vampire can only drink fresh blood."

"And sunlight will burn you," Eve said, looking at me. "Hey, your ears are back!"

I felt of my ears, and they had indeed grown back. "Drinking from Roland must have been enough to heal me."

"As Eve pointed out," I said to Dirkonus, "vampires are extremely sensitive to sunlight, but the blood we drink heals our wounds. You can also learn things from the people you drink from by entering their mind as if it were your own. That's how I was able to create that spear. I don't understand it completely, but I drank some kind of energy from another type of vampiric creature called a succubus. It didn't have a body like you and I, but was an apparition, much like the spear I made."

"Can I make a spear like that?" Eve asked.

"I'm not sure if the power is passed on that way," I answered. "Try to imagine it, and maybe you will be able to create one."

"You mentioned we could help each other," Dirkonus pointed out. "What did you mean by that? How can I help you?"

"Years ago, the city of Atronos was completely destroyed by giants, and the island of Crete was taken. An army was sent to take back the island but was no match against the giants. I believe a small army of vampires could destroy the giants, so humans can resettle Crete. What would you say if I made you my lieutenant in this immortal army?"

A smile spread across his face before he answered, "I've been dying to exact my vengeance."

"Then you will."

Still concentrating on summoning a weapon, Evelyn asked, "What about the elves?"

"We don't want their help," Dirkonus was quick to answer. "They can't be trusted."

"No, I mean, what if we learned some of their magic?" Eve clarified.

Nodding as I thought over it, I agreed with her. "That's a good idea, Eve. It's probably not a good idea to sneak into their hills since we don't know what we're up against, but perhaps we can go peacefully and ask for aid against the giants."

"That's crazy!" Dirkonus disagreed. "You're going to just walk up to their door and ask if you can drink some of their blood?"

"We don't have to tell them how we'll learn from them, just as we don't have to tell them we're immortal. Besides, I'd much rather ask the elves for aid than rush into battle, wielding sticks against giants," I told him, nodding at the spear he still held.

He took a deep breath and put the spear down. "Very well," he agreed. "We should get started then."

"So you're ready?" I asked him seriously.

"If I have to die to become immortal, then let's get it over with. I will leave the life of Dirkonus behind me."

"All right, Dirk," I called him before biting deep into my left arm. "Now, while I drink from your arm, you drink from mine."

"Why must you take my blood?"

"Because I will become too weak during the process if I don't," I explained, holding my wound tight with my hand. "Also, my blood will replace yours anyways."

I held my arm out to him, and he covered the wound with his mouth, ignoring the initial taste to gain my power.

"Drink until I tell you enough," I commanded. "Listen for my thoughts. You should be able to hear them soon."

I took his left arm and bit into it. I felt him tense beneath my fangs, but he continued to drink. Eve remained quiet, watching as I made another like us.

I began to see his memories, memories of his family being taken by giants while he was carried away by the river. He kept hold of the one thing that saved him, his brother's spear that was passed down from their father.

In case I needed to pass on my powers by thought, I began thinking of the short sword that I broke during my battle with the strigoi, and the ethereal sword that I was able to conjure afterwards. I thought of the other things I've done, like moving objects with an invisible force and putting someone to sleep while I drank from them.

I heard his heart tremble with the loss of blood, and his thoughts focused on drinking all he could until he lost consciousness, falling back on his bed of animal furs.

I applied pressure to my arm while I waited for him to come back. I looked at Eve and saw her holding a ghostly dagger with a big smile.

"You did it!" I said proudly.

She released her dagger and leaped into my arms, squeezing me tight. After hugging me, she sat in front of the fire with her head against my shoulder.

"Is it going to work?" she asked, looking at Dirk lying dead on his bed.

"It should. It just takes a few minutes for the blood to work its dark magic."

We sat for a moment in silence, listening to the crackling of wood burning. The smoke escaped through a small hole in the roof where we could see the cloudy afternoon was slowly becoming night.

Eve's loaf of bread was lying on the dirt floor next to the entrance. With her head still leaning against my shoulder, she extended a hand in an attempt to will the bread to her.

Without lifting a finger, I made the bread stand on its end. Eve gasped, thinking she moved it. She sat up straight and concentrated harder to bring the bread to her. I then waddled the bread to the door, pulled the animal skin back, and walked the bread outside.

She quickly turned to me. "You did that!" she fussed, slapping me on the leg.

I fell back against the wall of the hut, laughing while she hit me.

And then we heard it—the swelling, blood-thirsty cadence of Dirk's heart. His muscles twitched as my immortal blood rejuvenated every fiber, bringing him back from the nothingness beyond life.

He came up swinging before realizing where he was. Taking a deep breath to calm himself, he sat quietly, staring at his hands in the firelight.

"How do you feel?" I asked him.

Turning his eyes to me, he answered with a grin,

"Invincible."

CHAPTER IX

THE ELVES OF ASHWOOD

Dirk untied the bronze spear point from the wooden shaft and made a sheath for it from the fur he slept on. He tied it to his belt, and we traveled west to the Dark Hills, as they were called by the town's people.

During our hike through the dense forest, Dirk showed us some of his tracking skills. After spotting fresh droppings with his newly gifted vision, he searched the area and found tracks that led us to a herd of deer. I let Eve show him how we catch them. He loved that he was now quick enough to move in close for a kill.

It was just after midnight when an arrow in Dirk's left buttock warned us that we were dangerously close to the elves' home! We quickly took cover behind a large tree.

Stifling back her giggles, Eve pointed at the

arrow saying, "You got shot in the ass!"

Dirk pulled the arrow out with a grunt. Rubbing his wound, he said through a painful smile, "Yeah, a magic ass arrow."

I looked far into the forest, but even with my sharp, night vision, I couldn't see the shooter.

Suddenly, Dirk and I were both shot in the thigh!

"SHIT!" I cursed, pulling Eve around the tree before removing the arrow.

"There are at least three shooters," Dirk said to me, "and they're not together, so these trees won't help us for long."

Sensing another arrow coming through the trees, I threw up a hand, creating an ethereal shield to protect me and Eve from the shot. The arrow bounced harmlessly away.

"Come on," I told them, taking Eve's hand and running away from the unseen shooters.

Dirk followed us to another large tree where we took cover. "They're not trying to frighten us away. They're herding us toward the hills."

"Then we won't disappoint them. Can you both carry shields?" I asked.

Eve held out her little arm, tightening her fist. A ghostly round shield like mine formed. "Got it," she boasted.

Dirk and I found her attitude amusing.

"Well, let's go," she told us.

We laughed, and Dirk created a shield. More arrows came from both our left and right flanks, but we deflected them easily. We ran toward the Dark Hills ahead of us until we were stopped.

Three strange figures dropped from trees ahead

of us, brandishing swords that appeared frosted over. Three more ran up from behind us with bows drawn. They stood about five and a half feet tall, were clothed in animal furs, and had silvery black skin with white hair.

"Lower your shields," I commanded Eve and Dirk.

"Who are you, and why have you come so far into our realm?" one of the swordsmen asked.

"My name is Magnus. This is my daughter Eve and my son Dirk. Giants are taking our lands, killing our people. Unlike most humans, we three are capable of magic. We've come for knowledge of the arcane, so we may have an edge over our adversary."

The elves lowered their bows and sheathed their swords. "Then we have been expecting you," their speaker revealed. "My name is Torvin. Follow me."

"How did you know we were coming?" I asked. "Even we didn't know until yesterday."

"Your question will be answered soon enough."

The other five elves disappeared into the forest while he led us to a large, pitch black statue of two elves locked in combat, set into the hillside. He placed his hand on the statue and spoke in a strange tongue. To our amazement, the two stone elves began to move and stepped aside, allowing us to enter a tunnel into the hills.

We followed Torvin through a magically lit labyrinth of tunnels and were looked upon by the curious eyes of his people going about their business. We passed by large rooms where gemstones were being cut and weapons were being forged. We passed by other halls that were being mined. The long tunnel opened up to a wondrous dark forest with huts built in trees and along the forest floor.

"Welcome, humans, to the Dark Elven city of Ashwood."

I heard Eve say, "Wow!" under her breath at the beauty that our vampire eyes allowed us to see. Even the sky looked strangely different here.

Torvin led us down a series of stone steps and through the city. The ground was blanketed with moss, and mushrooms grew everywhere. We also saw flying creatures that looked like Dark Elves, only a few inches tall with soft, black wings.

Dirk swatted at one that flew too close to his face, but it easily dodged his swing.

"Easy," I told him, pushing his hand down. "We don't want to cause any trouble here."

"They're just curious," Torvin explained. "Most of them have never seen a human before."

"What are they?" Eve asked.

"They're Dark Fairies."

"They're so pretty," Eve said, holding her hand out to one. The fairy hesitantly touched one of her fingers and then quickly flew behind a tree to study us from a distance. "My name is Eve. What's yours?" she asked, keeping her hand out, hoping the fairy would return.

"It's all right," Torvin said to the tiny woman. "You can come introduce yourself."

We all remained still as the fairy flew out from behind the tree and stood in the palm of Eve's hand. "My name is Désirée," the fairy announced sweetly. She took hold of the hem of her violet dress and made a curtsey before flying in close to give Eve a kiss on the cheek. She then flew up into the trees, out of sight.

Continuing through the city, Torvin led us to the foot of a spiraling staircase that wrapped around a tree. "I will remain here while you speak with our Dragon Council representative," he told us. "Be not afraid, for he is both great and wise."

"Did he say dragon?" Dirk whispered to me.

With Eve holding both mine and Dirk's hand, we slowly walked single file up the staircase to a large hut that encompassed five trees. At the top of the stairs, we entered the center room which branched off to four others. Like in the labyrinth of tunnels, glowing crystals hung on the walls, illuminating the place.

Catching the scent of death, I looked into one of the rooms to see an elf boy, nearly Eve's age, examining a half-rotten goat carcass on his bedroom floor.

An old elf walked out of another one of the rooms to greet us. He looked to be nearly 60 years old with a patch over his right eye. He had long, white hair tied back into a ponytail, and his left eye was yellow. Like the other elves we've seen so far, he wore deer and rabbit furs.

"Well now, it's about time you show up!" the elf scolded me.

"Excuse me?" I asked the bitter old elf.

"I've been waiting on you for thousands of years!" he complained, waving us into one of his rooms.

I laughed as we followed him. "I don't know how old you are, sir, but I haven't lived that long."

"Sir?" he snarled. "Sir? I know who you are. Don't you know who I am?" he fired at us.

"Well, no," the three of us answered in unison, confused by his temperament.

"Oh, well then, perhaps I should introduce

myself; time's wasting you know. I am known as Ambrosius the Yellow, and this body that I inhabit is 591 years old next week," he answered.

"No way," Eve voiced in disbelief.

"Yes way, little lady," the elf said with a smile, stooping over to look her eye to eye.

Amazed, Eve asked, "Are you the oldest man alive?"

"Close, but not by a long shot," he answered, bringing a chuckle from us all.

"Your eye looks neat," Eve told him.

"Why, thank you. I can see the astral plane with it," he said, lifting the patch to show a blue crystal orb in the place of an eye.

Eve appeared disturbed by the sight it, for she had meant his healthy eye looked neat.

Standing straight, the old Dark Elf called for his boy. "Ambros!"

We heard a strange, throaty sound come from the boy's room and then a fast, tapping sound approach us. The boy galloped into the room, riding the dead goat that we saw him examining earlier. "I got it working, Pop! I got it working!"

"Gross," Eve cringed.

"It's pronounced 'goat,'" Ambros corrected her.

"No, it's definitely gross," Eve assured him.

"Ambros!" his father called again.

"Yes, sir," the boy snapped to attention, still sitting on the goat.

Pointing to Dirk, Ambrosius said, "Take, um, um," snapping his fingers, trying to conjure up his name without asking, "Dirkonus and um, Evelyn on a walk through the city."

"The name's Dirk," he told him.

"And Eve," she added her preference.

"Whatever," Ambrosius responded quickly, uninterested. "And leave that gross goat here," he told his son.

"Okay, Pop," he told his father, stepping off the putrid animal and leaving the room.

"Don't bite," I said to both Dirk and Eve with a nod that it was okay for them to see the city without me.

Eve gave me a disgusted look. "Who would want to?"

Dirk took her by the hand, and they followed Ambros to the stairs.

The boy's father snapped his fingers in front of the goat's face to get its attention, and then pointed to the door for it to leave. The animal did as commanded, going back to Ambros' room to wait for his return.

The room that we were in had a writing desk and stacks of scrolls everywhere. There was a long wooden rack on the wall that held various colored liquids, and a table littered with daggers and swords constructed with strange, crystal blades.

"Now, I suppose you have many questions," Ambrosius said, walking across the room to a doorway covered by an animal fur. He pulled the fur back for me to step outside onto a narrow porch where we could look out at the crystal lit tree huts of the city under the shimmering darkness of night.

Taking a seat in one of his wooden chairs, I opened my mouth to speak, but he cut me off.

"There's no need to ask them," he said, laughing, "but go ahead, Manius."

"I suppose I should start with the most obvious

question: Who in Hades are you?"

Pointing to himself, he answered, "I'm me, and you are you . . . at least for now."

"I mean, besides my wife, you're the strangest person I've ever met. How could you be expecting us? How do you already know our names? How was your son able to revive that decomposing goat? And what is up with the sky? I don't even know where to begin!"

Turning his sights upward, "What is up indeed? I believe the sky will answer that question when you are ready. As for your other questions, I can answer them but not easily."

"What do you mean?"

"We have a long road ahead of us, lad," he answered hesitantly. "A lot of it, neither of us are going to like, but it's what needs to be, you see?"

"No, I don't."

"You came here looking for power over your enemy, the giants, who have taken your lands and conquered your people, but it doesn't end there."

"How do you know this?" I asked him, shaking my head in disbelief.

"I am a sorcerer," he answered proudly. Standing from his chair, he propped up on the railing of the porch, looking off into the distance. "I have lived for millennia," he said.

"Wait. Wait," I stopped him. "You told Eve that you're 590."

"Ah," he said, turning to hold up a finger. "More precisely, I told her that this body I inhabit is 590. You don't think we start and stop with the flesh, do you?"

Without giving me time enough to answer, he said, "Oh, we are so much more than that, my friend, so much more. But, continuing with my story, my people and I took refuge in these hills during the Great Draconian Wars. We found traces of obsidian and metals, so we began mining. We tunneled into this dormant volcano, so we began bringing in dirt and planting trees where we built our homes."

"You mean to tell me this city is inside of a volcano?" I asked, thinking what a stupid idea it was. "What if it erupts?"

"I know when this volcano will awaken, and I can assure you that it won't be for some time."

"But how do you know? How do you receive this knowledge?"

"Through meditation," he answered. "I begin with the questions: What is it that I would like to know? Is the answer I'm looking for a cause or an effect? What direction through time should I travel to obtain the answer? Then, through meditation, I project myself and follow the path to knowledge, but the future has many paths."

"What do you mean by projecting yourself?"

"By leaving my body, I can cover unimaginable distances in a space unseen by our physical selves."

I was in awe. "May I have a demonstration of your power?" I asked of him.

"You'll soon see," he smiled.

"So what happened to your wife, if you don't mind me asking?"

His smile quickly faded before answering, "I never took a wife. I have always been considered too strange for anyone to love."

His answer caught me off guard. Confused, I asked, "Your boy isn't very old. Where is his mother?"

"He has no mother."

"But how is that possible?" I asked. "He had to have been born."

With a proud smile, he answered, "I made him. He is part of me, and at the end of our journey together, he will become me."

I couldn't even form a follow-up question to that. He saw from the tilt of my head that I was at a complete loss of words.

"Not all of us are lucky enough to be given eternal life," he laughed, patting me on the shoulder. "I realized during my first lifetime that one wasn't enough, so I began studying necromancy. I found that practicing necromancy may help me bring life back to a body, but it couldn't help me return its memories. Follow me." he said, walking back inside. "I'll show you something."

He led me to a room where he had a large, egg-shaped, green stone resting on a wooden pedestal. He removed the top of the stone to show that it had been cut, and the inside was hollow.

"I fill this green obsidian egg with a regen-erative elixir and submerge a particular part in order to duplicate myself," he explained. "It takes a full nine years to grow another me."

"Wow! The boy looks barely that old," I commented.

"Elves age differently from you humans."

"So your son, Ambros, is really you," I assumed.

"Not yet," he raised a finger. "Not until my consciousness is passed on to him."

"What part does this elixir call for?"

Ambrosius pointed at his eye patch.

My eyes involuntarily squinted. Just thinking

about it made them hurt.

"It's not a perfect process. I've made some alterations along the way, but it gets the job done," he told me, placing the top back on his crystal egg. "I keep better records of my life now; I lost so much work and so many memories the first few times I body jumped."

"What if I made you a vampire?" I offered.

"Thank you, lad," he smiled, "but that's not the path I wish to take. I do need your help though. I need you to be my vehicle into the far future and steer the course of history."

"And how do you suppose I do that?"

He took a seat and motioned for me to do the same. "There's a major event in time approaching, and certain things need to be set into motion which I myself cannot do."

"What is it that must be done?"

The elf picked up a long pipe that was on a table next to him, and with a simple rub of his fingers over the bowl, the contents began smoking. After taking a couple puffs from the smoking pipe, he told me an interesting tale.

"Since the dawn of the dragons, they have fought for supremacy. Each of their many races gathered armies of lesser creatures to use as pawns in wars to expand their territories. They came to be known as the Draconian Wars, and it was a truly terrifying age."

He took a few more puffs of his pipe, and the smoke he blew bellowed and took shape. Great and terrible dragons formed, filling the room. The smoke clouded out the crystal lights, but the room seemed ablaze with an otherworldly flame.

"After the death of the Dragon King," Ambrosius continued, "the Draconian Wars began to wane, and a small number of dragons met to discuss the direction of the world. After much debate, they agreed to share the earth under the condition that they rule together. They dispatched peacekeepers to the elven cities to protect them from outsiders and preach false hope that war was over. Few of us know the dragon lords' true objective."

"And what is that?"

"To constrict all the intelligent races to extinction," he answered with fear in his eyes.

"Why elves?" I asked. "Why bother giving them false hope of peace?"

"Because, with their king dead, we are the only ones the dragons fear can overthrow them. The dragon's so-called peacekeepers are nothing but a way to keep a close watch on us."

"So where is the dragon that spies on Ashwood? I was told I would meet with him."

With a sly grin and a proud puff of his pipe, he answered, "I have been giving reports under the guise of a dragon lord for many centuries."

"BAH! Orc shit!" I argued, standing quickly from my chair. "I may have witnessed some strange things, but I don't believe you can take the form of a dragon. So far, you've provided no proof that you have any sort of arcane ability. In fact, the only thing you do have is a little knowledge about me, a kid with a fetish for goats, and a weird eye!"

"You forgot to mention my fancy smoke tricks," he pointed out, smiling and taking a puff of his pipe.

Ambros came up the stairs and walked into the room, followed by Dirk and Eve.

"Come on. We're leaving," I told my companions, heading for the door.

"Do you know what time it is, vampire?" Ambrosius asked me.

The question stopped me in the doorway. I turned to look out a window. I could see that dawn hadn't yet come, but the night had indeed felt unusually long.

Now that he had my attention again, he sat his pipe down and stood from his chair, motioning for us to follow him to the porch. Looking up at the strangeness of the sky, it began to lighten to a shimmering blue that I've never seen.

"It's beautiful," Eve whispered.

"Where are we?" I asked, unable to look away from the sky. "What is this place?"

"The sun comes late and leaves early here," the boy explained. "The walls of the volcano block most of the light."

"There's a layer of obsidian high above us that filters the light when the sun is above us," his father explained further.

"Why does it shimmer the way it does?" Dirk asked.

"Over the millennia, rainfall has created a shallow lake, held above us by that thick layer of obsidian," Ambrosius answered.

"Amazing," I thought aloud.

"Here, let me show you amazing," the old elf said, grabbing hold of me and leaping over the railing of his porch!

Yellow, leathery wings sprouted from his back, and he carried me above the treetops where he then magically transformed into a huge Yellow Dragon! I suddenly felt tiny and foolish within his grip. He flew me up to the very ceiling of the city where I could see fish swimming above us! The lethal rays of the sun could not harm me beneath the blanket of obsidian.

He flew me back to the porch of his tree hut, returning to his normal size so not to damage his house.

"So," the sly, old elf began, "was that a proper demonstration of the power I wield?"

I didn't even grace his question with an answer. I merely smiled from ear to ear.

"We have an agreement then?"

"What agreement?" I laughed.

"Oh, I suppose I should tell you my plan," he laughed at himself for forgetting.

"It would be helpful," I agreed, sitting in one of the chairs.

Dirk and Eve were holding their hands out from the porch in the filtered sunlight. Curious what they were doing, Ambros held his hand out too but found nothing special about it. When they noticed that Ambrosius and I were watching them, they all took a seat.

"Like I said earlier," Ambrosius began, "the future has many paths, but I can give you an idea of what must be done." He stopped, looking at his empty hands and around him. "Ambros!" he called, leaning forward to see the boy sitting at the opposite end of the porch. "Fetch me my pipe. Will you please?"

"Yes, sir," Ambros responded.

"Thank you, my boy."

The old elf continued telling us his plan, but his boy didn't move from his chair. Instead, he cut his own finger with a knife and used the blood to draw strange markings on the floor between his feet. He then sat back in his chair and propped his feet up on the porch railing. He held his bloody finger out to Eve, who was sitting next to him, but she refused it.

"What I'll do," Ambrosius explained, "is report to the heads of the Dragon Council that I will be stepping down from my position and that you will succeed me. I will come back here where you'll drink my blood, absorbing my consciousness."

"But it doesn't work that way," I interrupted him. "I drink blood and learn things from my victims, but I don't absorb them."

"You will this time," he assured me, "and then you will have the powers needed to carry out your mission."

"And what is my mission?"

"I can't turn against my own people," he told me, keeping his voice down. "But it is the humans that should rule, not the dragons, not the elves. I have seen it."

I nodded that I understood.

We then heard the tapping sound of that undead goat approaching. It pushed its way through the fur covering the door and trotted over to Ambrosius, carrying his pipe in its rotting maw. I covered my mouth from sickened laughter. Ambrosius wasn't amused at all. He slowly pulled the disgusting pipe away from the rotting animal and threw it from the porch!

CHAPTER X

A DEAL WITH THE DEAD

For the next two weeks we stayed at Ambrosius' house while we waited for his return. Ashwood was a magnificent city and one where we could be outside during the day without having to dodge the sun. We left only when we needed a drink because we couldn't sneak around there like we could in human cities.

Eve grew to tolerate Ambros' bizarre behavior, and they even began playing together.

One afternoon, while sitting on the porch with Dirk, we overheard Eve and Ambros talking at the foot of the stairs.

Eve asked, "So do you like any of the girls here, like maybe Takarha?"

"No," he answered her. "She's too cold."

"What about Delanie? She seems nice."

"She's too sparkly."

There was quiet for a moment before I heard Eve ask, "Have you ever had a girlfriend?"

"No."

"Why not?" she asked curiously.

"Because none of them like me," Ambros admitted sadly.

"I like you," I heard Eve tell him, and it made me happy that she made a friend. I looked at Dirk, but he wasn't smiling.

"You shouldn't let them play together," he whispered.

"They're just kids," I argued.

"But we can't trust them."

"I'm sure they say the same about us."

"I don't care what they say about us. We shouldn't be here."

"We'll be on our way soon enough," I assured him.

"Welcome back, Pop!" I heard Ambros say.

"Thank you, son. I'm glad to be back."

Ambrosius had finally returned and came upstairs to inform us that all went as planned at the council meeting. All I needed now was Ambrosius' power to transform into a dragon and to introduce myself to the heads of the council.

With our children sitting on the porch, I followed Ambrosius into the room where he had the rack of potions.

"Are you ready?" I asked him.

"Not quite," he answered, taking two flasks from the rack. One contained a dark blue liquid. The other looked thick and yellow. "I would like a moment to speak to Ambros."

"Of course, I will get him for you."

Before walking outside to where our children were sitting, I watched him mix together the two liquids. The concoction began to foam green, and he quickly drank it down.

"Woo! That'll put hair on your feet," he commented, catching his breath.

I laughed and left the room to fetch his boy. When I stepped out on the porch that was built around the entire house, I saw Ambros trying to train his goat to carry a stick to Eve. Both Dirk and Eve were laughing at the boy's frustration. The goat merely stood there, staring and groaning at him.

"Your pop would like to speak to you," I told the young elf, taking a seat next to Eve.

"Then be that way!" he said to the goat before thanking me for relaying his father's request. He went into the house, followed closely by his putrid pet.

"Are you going to learn how to turn into a dragon?" my little girl asked me.

"Shhh," I quieted her. "I'd like to hear what Ambrosius has to say," I whispered.

We sat quietly but heard nothing. Minutes passed without a sound from inside.

"Do you hear anything?" Dirk finally spoke. "Because I hear nothing but dead silence."

I stood and walked to the door. Just as I was about to pull the animal hide back to look inside, Ambrosius opened it.

"What are you waiting for?" he asked me. "I'm ready to get this over with."

We sent our children and the goat to the foot of

the tree, so we wouldn't be distracted.

Ambrosius handed me one of his crystal knives. "It's important that you don't leave your usual mark, vampire."

"Is there anything else you would like to tell me before we do this?"

"I can't tell you what obstacles you'll face, but if you stay the course and do everything in your power to succeed, your people will rule this world."

"I will," I promised.

"And it may prove unwise to let another feed on you. You don't want my power in the wrong hands," he warned.

"I understand."

"Then um, do your thing," he directed, waving a finger at me.

Standing in his study, the old Dark Elf held his bare arm out to me. I sliced it without hesitation and put my mouth to the wound. I had gone without blood for too long, and I had been thirsting for power since I heard of the magic the elves possessed.

His blood tasted different from human. It ran cooler with a stronger metallic taste, but it brought life all the same. While I drank, I noticed the taste but not his memories. I searched his thoughts, but there was nothing. How could this be? The blood should be the key to access every facet of his being, but I was receiving no visions of his past, no thoughts of a lost love, no locations of other elf cities, and no knowledge of the arcane. I drained the elf dry, dropping his lifeless corpse to the wood floor.

Taking a moment to relax, I propped the elf's body up against the writing desk. I then sat on the floor across from it to think.

"What did I do wrong?" I asked myself.

"*Nothing*," Ambrosius' voice startled me.

I quickly looked at the body but saw no change. The elf's eye stared off blankly at nothing. His mouth was open, relaxed. His skin was dull and dry. I put my ear to his chest but heard nothing.

"Did you speak to me, Ambrosius?" I asked the dead elf.

When no answer came, I began to laugh. "Perhaps it was me. Perhaps I answered my own question. The question now is: What should I do with you? I can't leave your body here for your son to dispose of; that would be cruel."

I began pacing the floor. "I guess he could bring you back to life, but how would that help? You already said you couldn't return someone's memories, but . . . the undead king was somehow able to retain his identity."

"*Meditate*," I heard Ambrosius tell me. Again, I looked at the body and saw no change.

Instead of forcing myself to think, I did as the disembodied voice suggested. I sat down, closed my eyes, and let the thoughts come to me. Steady breathing and a clear mind quickly brought a vision from high above the trees. I was flying! My children looked small within red talons. I was a dragon! I saw where I should go and knew what I should do.

I opened my eyes to the dead body before me. "First, I need to get you out of Ashwood without drawing too much attention," I said to it.

I searched the house and found a large, grey quilt. I spread it out on the floor, placed Ambrosius' body on it, and rolled him up in it.

"Now, let's get you out of here quietly," I whispered, throwing him over my shoulder.

Looking around the room, I saw the stacks of scrolls containing untold knowledge. I'd like to sit down and study everything, but there's things I must do first. I'll have to come back.

I walked to the center room and began down the steps that circled the tree to find all of Ashwood sitting with candles. "So much for sneaking out quietly," I mumbled to myself. They all knew I carried their leader.

Torvin stood at the base of the tree with Ambros and my children. The rest of the populace formed a somber, candlelit road to the cavern leading out of the city.

Torvin kneeled before me. "Congratulations, Magnus, for becoming the newly appointed peacekeeper of Ashwood."

"Thank you," I acknowledged, bowing my head slightly. "How did everyone know?" I asked him, pointing to the rolled quilt over my shoulder.

Standing, Torvin told me, "Ambrosius foresaw this and prepared us for the coming change. For good or for ill, we all have a part to play in this grand adventure," he added, placing a hand on my shoulder.

Unsure of how to respond to his simple analogy of life, I gave an agreeing nod. "Will you be so kind to lead me and my companions out of the city?"

"Of course, my lord."

"When will you return?" Ambros asked Eve.

Looking to me for an answer, she asked, "Are we coming back?"

"If all goes well, I'll have her back in a couple

months," I told him, rubbing his head to mess up his neatly brushed hair. With long, silky white hair and yellow eyes, he indeed looked like a young Ambrosius.

He removed a necklace that he was wearing and handed it to Eve. It was made of wood, tiny skulls, and pieces of red, black, and green obsidian. "You can have this," he said bashfully. "I made it."

"It's pretty," Eve told him. "Thank you." She clasped the necklace on and hugged him.

"Goodbye friend," Ambros said sadly.

"Where are we going?" Dirk asked me.

"I'll tell you once we get out of the Dark Hills." Turning to Torvin, I told him to lead the way.

The elves of Ashwood sat quietly, each holding a candle as we passed. No one shed a tear. They paid their respects in silent.

Dark Fairies also carried little candles which made the sky appear filled with moving stars.

We left the city and passed through the caverns. Torvin opened the obsidian door for us and wished us a safe return.

"Make sure the boy is taken care of," I asked of him.

"Do not worry. He will be all right," Torvin assured me.

With it being late night, we were able to travel fairly quickly south east through the forest. Once we reached a good distance from the city, I began to tell Dirk my plan.

"During my travels with Vistilia, we came upon an ancient castle still inhabited by its rulers and their servants. The king of this castle held power over the dead."

"So what do you expect this king will do with a dead elf?" Dirk asked.

"The undead king wanted a fresh new body, so I'm bringing him one. If he can help us create an army to fight the giants, I may be able to strike a deal with him," I answered with a smile.

"Can we trust this undead king?"

I laughed, remembering how my previous visit turned out. "No, we can't, but we need his help."

We reached a clearing in the forest where I sat Ambrosius' body down, so I could concentrate.

"Are you going to turn into a dragon?" Eve asked excitedly.

"I'm going to try, Sunshine."

I stepped out into the center of the moonlit forest glade and raised my arms to the sky. I closed my eyes to look within for the power I needed. I imagined my body growing, taking a serpentine form. My heart rate quickened, and my breathing became heavy. I felt the change come over me like a tornado touched down. I opened my eyes to find myself as tall as the surrounding trees! I was a dragon, and I was a delicious crimson color. I turned to see Dirk and Eve staring up at me in utter amazement.

"I think it's time I return to the undead king's castle," my voice thundered.

I reached down to carefully pick up my children. Eve raised her arms, ready to go.

"I'm sick of walking," she said with a big smile on her face.

"What about the body?" Dirk asked me.

I thought I would have to carry Ambrosius' corpse in my mouth, but then I noticed I could grip with my hind talons, so that's how I carried it. I didn't have much room to spread my wings, now that I was a dragon, but it didn't take much to clear the treetops where I could take flight.

The cool night air in my face felt amazing, and my dark children seemed to enjoy it too.

"Higher! Higher!" Eve yelled.

Beating my powerful wings, I climbed higher into the clear night sky.

"Dive! Dive!" she then yelled.

Thinking of how a hawk dives for its prey, I pulled my wings in and pointed my head down. I felt Eve and Dirk holding on tight within my grasp and heard them scream with excitement. Before plunging into the forest below us, I extended my wings and pulled up to gain altitude. I heard Eve scream, loving the maneuver, but it was Dirk who lost his lunch! Both, Eve and I laughed at him, but I was careful not to cause him to throw up blood on me again.

It didn't take nearly as long to return to the king's ancient castle. Entering the courtyard brought back memories of the last time I was there, several weeks earlier. Vistilia was with me then. I wished she was with me now; I was beginning to miss her.

I gently placed the rolled quilt on the ground before landing. Sitting my children down, I returned to my human form.

"That was so fun," Eve commented before looking at me and turning away quickly.

"Um, Magnus," Dirk began with a straight face, "your clothes didn't change with you."

I then realized I was completely nude! "By Charon's ship!" I cursed. "I'm sorry, Eve. Just give me a moment, both of you."

Dirk turned his back to me while I unrolled Ambrosius and took his robe.

Eve looked around at where I brought her. It was an ancient castle surrounded by dead trees. "This place is scary," she commented.

"Wait till you see inside," I told her, throwing the wrapped body over my shoulder to carry into the depths of the castle.

"As long as this corpse king remains clothed, he shouldn't be all that scary," Dirk joked.

"Funny," I mocked as I walked past them. "Eve, please hold on to your brother's hand."

"You don't have to tell me twice," she answered, taking his hand and following me into the crumbled walls of the castle.

"And don't break your brother's fingers," Dirk said, laughing at the grip she was putting on him.

The large stones that I used to seal the entrance had been cleared. I cautiously peeked over into the hole where Vistilia and I had entered, half expecting to be attacked again by the centurions. After taking one last breath of fresh air, I dropped into the hole with Ambrosius' body over my shoulder.

"WELCOME BACK," the dead walls greeted cheerfully.

I responded with a lackluster, "Thank you. I'm thrilled to be back."

"What's down there?" I heard Eve frightfully ask from above.

"It's all right, Sunshine," I answered. "You can come on down."

The walls began stirring and the dead peeled

away, receding farther down the corridor. "HE BROUGHT THE SUN WITH HIM! HE MEANS TO DESTROY US!"

Dirk dropped in next to me, holding Eve. "You scared them off," he told her.

"Good," Eve said with a smile.

"They're right to run because you stink," Dirk added, fanning his nose.

Eve slapped his arm. "That's not me! I don't stink!"

We laughed and began walking down the long corridor. The bodies that covered the walls stayed far ahead of us, but their stench saturated everything.

The undead king and queen were sitting high on their throne of the deceased. The walls and ceilings writhed with bones and gore.

"Ah, Magnus, you have returned," the king said happily, reminding me of his unnerving voice as we entered the room. "I hardly believed them when they said you had, especially since they claimed you were bringing sunshine down upon us. HAGH! HAGH! HAGH!" his laugh sounding like a hoarse cough.

"WE THOUGHT YOU WERE THE SUN!" the collective dead said, pointing many fingers at Eve.

"No, I'm the daughter," Eve clarified, bringing a stumped silence from the talkative dead.

While holding the rolled quilt steady with one hand, I placed my free hand on Eve's shoulder and introduced her to them. "This young lady is my sunshine, Eve, and this is Dirk."

The queen rose from her thrown and floated quickly down to us. "Such a delightful little girl," she commented.

Dirk pulled Eve close to him but said nothing.

The queen hissed. "I'm not going to harm the child." She backed away, and before returning to her seat, she asked me, "Magnus, where is your exquisite wife?"

"She . . . needed some time away," I answered.

"That's a shame," the queen commented. "She had such magnificent skin. You both ran away before we could properly introduce ourselves."

"That's because you tried to kill us!" I reminded them.

Both the king and queen laughed.

"We just wanted to replenish these dry, crumbling bodies," the king admitted, examining the decayed flesh of his hands.

The queen took his hand in hers, bringing him from his thoughts.

"Ah yes," he said. "Sir Magnus, I am King Byron, and this is Queen Hela. Now that I've properly introduced us, let's see this body you have over your shoulder."

I placed the grey quilt gently at the foot of the throne and unrolled the nearly nude cadaver.

Byron stood from his chair and floated down for a closer look. He recognized the race immediately. "A Dark Elf!" he said excitedly. "Where did you find him?"

Ignoring his question, I told him, "I need an army of soldiers like the centurions you summoned against me."

Staring at the body for a moment, he then said, "Bring him over here."

I picked up the body and followed him to the back of the throne room where the dead on the walls divided to reveal another room. There were many shelves holding scrolls, tablets, and jars containing body parts and organs. In the center of the room, there was a table with a corpse on it.

"Get off the table!" King Byron commanded, slapping the edge of it.

To my amazement, it did as it was told. The corpse stood up and scuffled into the throne room where it was absorbed into the mass of decaying flesh on the wall.

I placed Ambrosius' body on the table, so Byron could examine it. He removed the eye patch and pried the blue obsidian orb from the eye socket. He looked at the arm where I had bled him dry.

"Other than the missing eye and the blood loss, I like this body," Byron told me. "I have plenty of spare eyes looking around here, but I don't have any Dark Elf blood."

"Can you use this body without the blood?" I asked him.

"I can, but it will soon begin to waste away like my current body," he explained. "You mentioned you need an undead army. May I ask who you plan to march against?"

Choosing my words carefully, I told him what he needed to know. "I am a newly elected member of the Council of Dragons, but I do not share their vision of the future. The world belongs to the humans, dear king. All others must be eliminated, starting with the giants of Crete."

"You, Magnus, are a dragon?" Byron asked in disbelief.

"I wear a deceptive guise, do I not?" I questioned with a wily grin. I ran my fingers through my dark hair, changing it to red. I blinked and showed him red, reptilian eyes to better sell the deception.

"I sense you conceal many surprises," he voiced through a broken smile.

"Only the important ones," I laughed.

"Indeed. Well, many bodies are needed for an army large enough to conquer the world, my friend," Byron expressed his doubt in my plan.

"But you and your centurions have a great advantage that no other army can match," I explained. "You're already dead."

"Yes, every enemy we kill becomes another soldier under my command," he stated proudly.

"Then what has stopped you from marching against the armies of the world and ruling it with an undead fist?" I asked him.

"You," he shrieked, startling me. "The dragon lords command a terrible army. That's how my castle was destroyed," he revealed. "My forces were growing strong, and my territory was expanding with each new conquest. The council only needed a few dragons to decimate my centurions and overthrow me."

I sat on the edge of the table before telling him my battle plan. "Instead of marching against the giants, what if I flew just you and Dirk to Crete where you can raise the humans that were killed? There must be hundreds all around their camps."

"What if this plan of yours fails?" he asked, examining the palms of Ambrosius' hands.

"It won't. I have foreseen our victory," I assured him.

"This elf did not suffer from the hardships of

living alone in the wild. He lived within a city," Byron surmised. "If you tell me the location of this Dark Elf city, I'll summon your army."

A smile crept over my face as I shook King Byron's dismal hand.

CHAPTER XI

THE COUNCIL OF DRAGONS

High above the clouds, I soared. The sense of freedom was indescribable. I had left Eve and Dirk at the town near Byron's castle until I returned. I didn't fly to meet with the council though. No, not yet. I flew back to Ashwood to get Ambros out of the city. I may be given the task to eliminate all the races that threaten humanity, but I would not see this little elf become a centurion in Byron's undead army.

I wished Vistilia were with me. Even though I was in the form of a dragon, she would have laughed at me for having to fly naked. "HAHAHAA!" I laughed aloud from my amusing thoughts. I certainly couldn't stop by Ashwood or show up for an important meeting naked, so I kept a firm grip on my clothes for when I arrived.

I returned to my human form and dropped down

into the Dark Hills where I soon met with Torvin and the other elves that protected the surrounding forests.

After receiving a courteous bow from each of them, I told Torvin, "I've come to see Ambros."

"My apologies, Lord Magnus, but Ambros is no longer here," he informed me. "Like he did with us, Ambrosius prepared his son for the coming future, only he is set on a different path."

"Do you know where he may have gone?"

"No," he smiled. "We are not supposed to know."

"Very well," I nodded.

"Is there anything else I can assist you with, my lord?"

"No, thank you. I shall see you again soon." With a bow, I leaped above the forest before extending leathery wings.

I flew east, but I didn't have to see the lay of the land to know where I was going; I could feel the direction of my destination. The earth far below me was a beautiful, lush, green landscape of rolling hills and towering mountains. It looked so different from this altitude. It seemed peaceful and perfect.

With the speed that I could now travel, I arrived at my destination just before dawn. Hidden away in a valley, I found a palace under construction. Few were out working on it at this early hour, but there were many tents set up around the area and large blocks of marble set aside for the project. With construction already well underway, it was clear that this palace would be like nothing the world has ever seen.

I landed at the edge of the site where there were no tents for the force of my wings to disturb. I took my human form but decided to wear the same subtle disguise of red, reptilian eyes and red hair that I showed Byron.

I walked to the encampment. A large fire pit was being tended to by two men. As I approached, I noticed they both had pointy ears like the Dark Elves of Ashwood, but they had a fair complexion in the firelight.

"A pleasant sunrise to you, sir," one of the elves said to me with a bow while the other was busy throwing wood onto the fire.

"Have the other council members arrived?" I asked.

"They've been here since construction began on the palace," he answered, noticing my red eyes. "They are already at the ancient Dragon Cavern," he told me. "You should head on in and not delay." He then pointed up to a large cave on the side of a mountain.

I thanked him and ran through the construction site. I leaped into the air and transformed into a dragon, so I could fly up to the cavern entrance.

The mouth of the cave was large enough to enter as a dragon, so I kept my form and ventured inside. Down, down, I crawled into the heart of the mountain where four great dragons sat around a large stone table in an illuminated cavern. One of the dragons was sleek black. Another was snow white. There was one that was a magnificent golden yellow. The fourth had very distinct brown markings and five heads! This winged serpent had two sets of arms but no legs.

The five-headed dragon slithered over to me and held two of his palms up to me. Slowly, I placed my hands on them. He bowed his heads slightly. "A splendid dawn to you," his middle head, which stood the tallest of the five, greeted me.

"Thank you," I bowed. "A splendid dawn to you."

"You must be Magnus the Red. Welcome," the strange dragon's head second from the left said.

"I am."

"We can't see your thoughts," the far right head admitted.

"You must have a powerful mind indeed to keep us locked out," the adjacent head finished.

"I'm sorry," I smiled, thinking it was best they not see my thoughts.

The head farthest to the left said, "There's no need for apologies."

"Ambrosius' mind was locked to us as well," the head second from the right disclosed.

"He would sense when we were trying to hear his thoughts," the center head admitted.

"And tell us that we were invading his privacy," the head to its right added, bringing a laugh from them all.

"But where are our manners?" the center head apologized. We are Grimlash, the heads of the council." He turned to the Black Dragon and motioned for him to introduce himself.

Holding his head high, "I am Valik the Black Dragon Lord," he said with a thick accent.

The White Dragon then bowed courteously saying, "I am Elsbareth the White Lord of the Cold Mountains." Her voice, on the other hand, was very articulate.

"And I am Assim, the newly appointed Lord of

the Yellow Dragons," he introduced himself with a bow. "Welcome."

"Once the palace is finished," Grimlash said, returning to his place at the table, "we will have a lavish meeting room. Until then, we'll meet here in the Dragon Cavern where the council has met for millennia."

I sat at an empty space across from Grimlash between Valik and Assim so the meeting could resume.

"To get you caught up, we'll quickly go over what's going on in the world and the actions this council is taking to direct it," Grimlash said to me. With his heads each taking a turn speaking, he began, "The world, as you know, is home to many intelligent creatures, far more than it can sustain for any lengthy amount of time without conflict. The Dragon Council was formed, not only to dissolve the tension between the dragon clans, but to restore order to our lands. In recent years, though, the increasing population and number of conflicts reveal our increasing loss of control. The former council leader merely followed his predecessor's campaign of maintaining peace between the races, but if we don't act now, we will lose our world forever."

"How will we put an end to the conflicts and restore order?" Assim asked our council leader.

"Ambrosius the Yellow, who had been a council member for many centuries, advised that we urge all our kin to get involved, so we will, without fail, regain control. A place where we can all live and operate from would be the most efficient way to bring this plan together. We will then do what we should have done from the beginning: Turn the intelligent races against one another. Why police the entire world forever when eliminating the cause would solve the problem? With a legion of dragons under our command, we should mold this world the way it ought to be molded. We," he stressed, "will be the only intelligent race of this world. Harmony will be restored," he preached.

"Harmony restored," both Valik and Elsbareth repeated strongly.

It seemed the plan that Ambrosius informed me of was far more severe than he led me to believe. If I could keep my true identity and my team secret, perhaps I could turn their plans against them.

"We have already set the race of Giants against Man," Grimlash revealed.

Anger swelled within me like a terrible heat! The taking of Crete and the destruction of my home was not just the territorial expansion of giants, but it was ordered by these dragons, by Grimlash!

He then turned to the Black Dragon Lord, "Valik, is there anything you would you like to add?"

Focusing his thoughts through his hands, Valik created an illusion of tiny mountains, forests, and oceans that filled the entire stone slab before us. Three large areas of the map were colored red.

"I have personally overseen the three tribes to guarantee their success," Valik began. "The red areas represent the regions where giants have seized control. We were met with strong resistance here," he pointed to the red area directly in front of me. "It is an island the humans call Crete."

Crete! Atronos! My family! My home! My blood boiled, but I remained calm, so I could save to memory the regions that the other giants inhabited.

"The race of Giants may teeter on the brink of extinction," Valik explained, "but with my leadership and the promise of prime hunting grounds, they remain a formidable force."

"Once their usefulness has expired, though, they can be easily dispatched," Grimlash added.

Sitting across the table from Valik, Elsbareth pointed to an area far north of Crete. "I have been aiding the race of goblins by carrying small numbers of them from their homelands to the farthest reaches of the world," she boasted. "Where giants take land by force, goblins overtake it in sheer numbers. And unlike giants, goblins are far from extinction. They are surprisingly resourceful, and like water on stone, they only need time to make an area their home."

"Thank you, Elsbareth," Grimlash bowed.

"How easy would it be to exterminate these goblins?" I asked the council, but my question brought a laugh from them.

"The goblins are an ancient race as old as or older than we are," Grimlash informed me. "They pose no threat to the likes of us, but they do make tasty snacks."

It was now Grimlash who brought a hearty laugh from his council members. Even I laughed at his witticism.

"I noticed you have many Woodland Elves here for the construction of the palace," Assim mentioned. "Will they be among the races that we eliminate?"

"Yes," Grimlash answered, "but they don't know that, and we should keep it that way. The elves are the only real threat that we face. They may not have the numbers of the goblin race or even the Human race, but they hold an immense knowledge of the arcane arts," he explained. "We've encouraged them to get involved with the building process, so we're calling it the World Council Palace instead of the Dragon Council Palace, so they will think they're helping with the transition of power."

Suddenly, I realized why Ambrosius suggested the idea of bringing the race of Dragons to one location. Perhaps I could build on that model. If we helped the elves build a large city so they are less scattered throughout the forests, we could then destroy them in one swift stroke.

"We will meet again during the next new moon," Grimlash announced. "Once the other dragons arrive, we will lay out our plan to purify the world. In the meantime, you and Magnus must assist the giants until time for our meeting." He then motioned that Assim and I were free to leave.

"Very well, my lord," Assim bowed.

I said nothing. I gave a simple bow and left the meeting chamber behind Assim. At the mouth of the large cavern, we stopped. It was a dreadfully sunny day, so I needed to find shelter from the sun.

Assim turned to me before leaving, and with a silent message that I heard without him uttering a word, he said, *"I believed I could make a difference in the world by joining this council. I believed I could restore the peace that I've heard tales of. I feel that the heads of the... Well, now isn't the time for this kind of talk,"* he stopped himself. "Sea Giants dwell on and around the island of Crete," he said aloud. "The Storm Giants' region is to the far north from there, and the Fire Giants' is to the east. How about we part ways?" he asked. "I will go aid the Storm Giants while you aid the Sea Giants. Then we can meet up in the realm of the Fire

Giants."

"That would be best," I answered, thinking to myself, I will aid the Sea Giants all right. I will aid them to the doorstep of Hades, so they may be cast into the depths of Tartarus.

"It was nice to meet you, Magnus the Red. May your journey be successful," Assim said with a bow.

"Thank you. And it was nice to meet you, Assim the Yellow," I mimicked his courteousness. He then left the cave, spread his wings, and headed west to one of the giant encampments. He looked all the more brilliant under the mid-day sun, like his serpentine form was malleable gold.

I couldn't leave the way he did, not with the sun bearing down, so I took human form and quickly ran from the cavern to the shade of the trees on the mountain side. I made my way to the campsite of the palace builders and waited in one of the tents for dusk.

While I impatiently paced the floor, I heard someone approaching. There was nowhere to hide, so I sat on a trunk full of clothing. A Woodland Elf stepped in.

Noticing my dragon eyes, she promptly bowed. "My lord," the elf said, surprised that one of the Dragon Council members was in her tent. "How may I be of assistance?"

With a devilish grin, I said, "Actually, I came in to get out of that dreadful sun, but since you're here, I could use a thirst quenching drink."

Before she could say another word, I grabbed her, covering her mouth so she couldn't scream! I felt the tender skin of her neck break beneath my bite, and her deliciously sweet life did, in fact, quench my thirst.

Through her thoughts, I found that Woodland Elves can speak to animals. Now, I can speak to animals.

This wasn't the place to leave a corpse, so I didn't kill her. I drank only what her body would allow before placing her gently on the bed.

"Thank you, my dear," I said, sitting next to her. I bit my tongue and licked the wound I had left on her neck so the skin would heal quickly. She would be unconscious for a while and will wake up with no memory of me. I still had a bit longer to wait before sunset, so I focused on searching the elf's mind for more abilities.

I gently combed her dark brown hair away from her face. "Well hello, Larisa," I said to the unconscious elf once discovering her name. She appeared to be in her mid-thirties, but her mind told me she was 341! She was there with her mate. They were actually brought by Assim to make clothing.

"Now, that's an ability that will come in handy," I said to myself. "You weave them from magic! Thank you, Larisa. Thank you very much."

After noticing the lack of sunlight through the fabric of the tent, I knew it was finally time for me to be on my way.

CHAPTER XII

THE SEA GIANTS

I left the campsite and flew directly back to the village where I had left Eve and Dirk. I found them sitting in Bilford's Bread, Brew, & Bedding.

Eve ran to hug me. "Hi, Sunshine," I said to her.

"Welcome back," Bilford greeted me. "I was afraid the strigoi may have gotcha," he said with a jolly laugh.

"No. Not today," I chuckled.

"So what are we havin' this evening, good sir?"

"I need a room for this little lady."

"Very well."

"Be sure she is kept safe, will you?"

"I will," he answered. "Those bloodsuckin' bastards won't come into this place, if they know what's good for 'em." He reached under the counter and brought out a sword and four small daggers sheathed on a belt.

I listened to his thoughts. He meant to keep his word. He did not suspect that we were vampires, the very creatures he once hunted.

Dirk handed Bilford some money to pay for the room.

Eve pulled my arm, wanting to whisper something to me, so I bent down to listen.

"But I want to go with you," she whispered, glancing at Bilford to see if he was listening.

"I'm sorry, Sunshine, but you're not a soldier," I explained to her.

"But didn't you make me faster and stronger? I want to help," she pleaded.

"You are faster and stronger, and I know you want to help, but I'm not sure what we're getting into," I told her honestly. "This will be too dangerous for you, and I don't want you to get hurt."

"Okay," she said sadly, holding her head down.

I kissed her on the forehead and told her, "Now remember: Don't drink from anyone. If you get thirsty, go into the forest and catch something. When Mr. Bilford gives you food, take it outside with you. You must keep what we are a secret."

"I will," she acknowledged.

"Don't venture too far from the village, and stay away from Byron's castle," I warned.

"Believe me; I don't want to go back to that smelly place."

Dirk walked over, so we could get the mission underway. "The castle probably smells like daisies now that you're not there," he joked.

Eve slapped his stomach. "I told you, I don't

stink!"

We hugged her goodbye, and we were on our way.

I had chased the sun west from my meeting with the council, so we still had an entire night ahead of us to begin our attack on the Sea Giants of Crete.

Dirk and I ran up the mountain trail to Byron's castle.

"I don't like the idea of rushing into a fight without first seeing exactly what we're up against," Dirk told me.

"I don't like it either," I agreed, "but we don't have much of a choice. The ships of Athens couldn't even make land before they were sunk. Of course, if our attack doesn't go well, I'll have to get us out quickly, but the visions I saw revealed that we will succeed."

"Well, that's encouraging to know."

We reached Byron's castle to find a familiar Dark Elf sitting on one of the broken stone pillars in the courtyard.

"Ambrosius," I called, "or shall I say, King Byron?" I reached out to shake his hand.

"This was once the flesh of Ambrosius, but it belongs to me now," Byron said with a big smile, shaking my hand.

He even had Ambrosius' voice, instead of the frightening voice of the dead that he had before. I noticed that he wasn't wearing an eye patch either. His yellow eye was the same as before, but in place of the blue obsidian orb, there was a working blue eye.

"I see you have replaced the eye. Were you also able to replace the blood?"

"I know the colors don't match, but a true yellow

eye is hard to come by. I pulled this replacement from one of my centurions, and no, I have not acquired blood yet," he answered. "This body requires the blood of a Dark Elf, so for now, magic fuels it. It is a superb body to inhabit though," he commented, examining his arms and stretching his fingers. "It is far better than any human's. Thank you."

"You're very welcome," I said with a bow before asking if we were ready to go. After a silent nod from both Dirk and Byron, my muscles tensed, and a whirlwind of magical energies transformed my body from human to Red Dragon.

Dirk asked with a laugh, "Were you going to carry a change of clothes, or will we have to ignore your naked ass on the battlefield?"

I let out a thunderous laugh before answering, "Be thankful, my son, for I have solved that problem."

With a snap of my fingers, I used my newly acquired spell to magically change his old clothing into a new set of leather armor.

"Nice trick," Byron commented.

"Amazing! Thank you," he said, tapping against his chest.

"What about for you, Byron?"

"Nothing for me, thank you," he answered. "I prefer my own clothing."

"Very well."

I then carefully lifted him and Dirk with my front claws before taking flight. I flew south to my homeland. I suppressed the exhilaration and dread of war that flooded my thoughts, so I could focus on what I must do. Using the clouds as cover, I crossed the Mediterranean to Crete. I flew over the large island and saw that there were several camps, but it seemed all the giants were concentrated at a single campsite on the northwestern shore.

While still high in the sky, I asked Byron, "Are you able to sense the deceased even if their bodies are buried?"

"Yes," he answered. "Just release me outside their village. Whether I find the bodies of giants or humans, I'm sure I'll find something to work with."

"Good." I then dove from the clouds to the forests of Crete. I sat my army of two on the ground and watched Byron walk away slowly with his eyes closed and his hands out. "Do you sense anything," I asked him.

"Oh yes. There was so much glorious death here," he answered joyfully.

"Mind your tongue, sorcerer," I expressed my disapproval before remembering I had a deception to sell.

Byron stopped to apologize. "Forgive me, Lord Magnus."

"We must not take joy in our enemies' accomplishments," I said to hide my error. I attempted to read his thoughts to see if he suspected me as anything but a dragon, but saw nothing. His mind was too powerful for me to access, and it would do no good to bite him since he had no blood for me to follow to his thoughts. I had to assume my ruse endured and mind my own tongue.

"Watch after Byron while he assembles the army," I commanded Dirk. "I am going to meet the Sea Giants."

"Yes, sir," he acknowledged.

"And don't take too long," I ordered Byron. "I'm sure you wouldn't want to be stranded here to face an army of giants alone."

"You're quite right," he answered with wide eyes. "I will not disappoint you."

I leaped into the air and flew to the giant's encampment on the beach not far away. The human-like creatures lumbered out to greet the dragon in their midst. I listened to their thoughts, but all I ascertained was a primitive language of grunts and growls. They ranged from ten to fifteen feet tall. They had slick, dark green skin with gills along their necks so they could also breathe underwater. They were sparsely clothed in smooth animal hides, probably cut from a particular undersea creature. They were armed with spears that had manmade swords roped to the tip.

Two giants that were no doubt their leaders stepped ahead of the others to speak to me. One was definitely a different breed of Giant. Standing at nearly twenty feet tall, he had pale, blue skin and carried a ceremonial staff that looked more like a wand within his massive hands. The giant that accompanied him was an elderly looking Sea Giant clothed in many animal hides. From their thoughts, I knew they were intelligent enough for us to communicate.

"Welcome, great dragon," the Sea Giant leader said, and all the giants kneeled before me.

I listened for the sound of an undead army approaching from the forest, but I heard nothing. Should I begin the fight without them, or should I maintain this deception until they arrive? There are three hundred or more giants here, so I shouldn't be too hasty.

"I am Magnus the Red Dragon Lord of the

World Council," I announced.

The giants stood and their leader spoke. "Thanks to Lord Valik and a single Storm Giant from the north, we were able to crush the puny humans of Crete."

Anger boiled within me like I felt at the council meeting! I clenched my teeth and remained quiet so that I wouldn't give away my true intentions so soon.

The Sea Giant leader continued, "Lord Valik informed us that he or another council member would be sent to relay our next orders. Our entire force is at your command, my lord."

He waved a hand to present his soldiers. In unison, they all plunged a fist into the air and yelled.

"Where shall we strike next?" the Sea Giant asked.

I listened again for Byron's army but still heard nothing.

"My lord," the aging leader asked again, "what is your command?"

This is the chance for revenge that I've always hoped for. I will not let Byron's failure keep me from doing what I came here to do. I am finally face to face with the monsters that killed my father, murdered my people, and destroyed my home. My anger boiled so hot that I felt it in the back of my throat. I could no longer contain it, so I unleashed it upon my enemies as a roaring blast of fire!

Dozens of Sea Giants, including their leader, were immediately turned to ash within my fiery breath! The Storm Giant, however, was able to shield himself. Once I exhaled all the air from my lungs, I took to the sky to escape the spears that were being thrown at me. I pulled one from my side before circling around to breathe fire along the entire length of their encamp-ment. Many spears were thrown but most missed their mark. I did feel a couple spears penetrate my leathery wings, but that wasn't enough to keep me out of the sky. I turned and made another pass along the beach, burning everything I could.

A bolt of lightning, sent from the Storm Giant's staff, locked around my left leg as I passed over! My jaws clamped shut, and my body stiffened as electricity popped and crackled along my scales. The Storm Giant then yanked me out of the air, and I fell hard on the beach. Before I could get to my feet, the clever giant charged over and struck me across the face with his staff. I involuntarily returned to my human form.

"A human!" the Storm Giant yelled out, now towering over me on the beach.

Howls of rage roared out along the beach from the surviving Sea Giants that quickly surrounded me, and I feared I was about to find out just how immortal I really was.

A long spike of ice formed at the tip of the Storm Giant's staff. Just when he was about to plunge it into my chest, an entire legion of corpses flooded the beach to consume the flesh of my enemies!

I scrambled away from my captor while he fought off the zombie onslaught. With an invisible hand, I tried to pull his magical staff away from him. The break in his attacks allowed the zombies to overwhelm him, and I was finally able to wrench the staff from his grip.

As the giant struggled against the relentless zombies, I threw the staff, and it pierced his throat with the spike of ice that was intended for me! He pulled the staff from his neck but toppled to the sand where zombies tore the flesh from his bones.

I limped over to the monster and drank from him. The zombies didn't seem to mind sharing with me. I saw memories of Valik bringing him there many years earlier to aid the Sea Giants. I saw he was also the giant who decimated the Athenian ships before they reached shore. I drank more to understand his control over the staff he wielded and learned how to build an electrical resistance, so my body would naturally push lightning away.

The beach was now littered with dead giants and Byron's apparently starving, zombie army. I saw a few of the surviving giants trying to escape into the ocean, so I used the magical staff to stop them. I plunged it into the sand at the water's edge. The water began to freeze, trapping the giants before they could escape. Zombies slipped across the ice to get to the trapped giants.

Byron and Dirk stepped out of the forest, and the three of us burst into laughter. Relief washed over me with our victory.

Examining my leg, I saw that I had burns all the way to the bone from where I was lashed with lightning. I also had the terrible scent of scorched flesh in my nose that I couldn't immediately rub out.

"Well, that seemed easy enough," Byron commented.

I laughed at his remark. "But you didn't get struck by lightning," I said, showing him my wounded leg.

"Ah, that's nothing," he blew. "I can get you a new leg when we get back."

"Um, no thanks."

"So what would you like me to do with the army?" Byron asked me.

With nothing left for them to eat, the zombies wandered slowly along the beach.

"Dispose of them. Have them carry the giant's remains into the ocean," I told him, pulling the staff from the sand.

The warm waters of the Mediterranean quickly chipped away at the frozen shoreline until there was nothing but chunks of ice melting in the surf.

"Very well," he answered, and his army immediately obeyed.

It seemed fitting that, not just me, but the fallen people of Crete exacted revenge on the giants that took our land, I thought to myself as I watched the undead carry the dead past the surf, into the deep.

With waves washing up around our feet, I presented the Storm Giant's staff to Byron for his assistance. He couldn't wait to study its magical properties.

While we walked through the torch lit camp looking for other artifacts that could be useful, we saw that the giants had collected a lot of treasure during their attacks. There were crates stacked on top of crates full of gold nuggets and precious stones!

"Too bad we can't carry it all back with us," Dirk said sadly.

"Why not bury it?" Byron suggested. "Then, you can come back to get it whenever you like."

A shining smile from us both was enough of an answer to Byron's question. "Hold this a moment," he said, handing me his staff. Pressing his knuckles together, he closed his eyes to concentrate. His hands began shaking, and he slowly began pulling them apart. To our amazement, the ground ripped open. "Quickly," he said. "Push them in."

Dirk grabbed a couple handfuls of gold to put in his pocket. Then, he and I tossed all the crates into the deep crevasse before Byron closed it up.

"I don't think anyone will find that," Dirk said. He offered Byron half of the gold that he kept, but Byron waved it away.

"What does a necromancer need with a handful of rocks?"

Shocked that he didn't want them, Dirk said, "These are worth a fortune!"

"BLAH! The currency of mortals," he spat. "I deal in powers beyond the realm of the physical. Do you honestly believe that the world around us is comprised of only the things you see with your own two eyes?"

"I prefer to stay grounded in the reality that I'm familiar with," Dirk said to him.

"Reality is far more expansive than you realize, young one. If you open your mind, you will see that knowledge is the real treasure."

After changing into a dragon, I interrupted their conversation. "If we're done here, I'd like to be heading back."

"Yes, Lord Magnus," Byron answered.

I carefully took hold of them and flew us to Athens, where I told the night guardsmen to inform their king that the Sea Giants have been defeated, and Crete could be resettled. Of course, I didn't approach the city in the form of a dragon; I didn't want to cause a panic.

I then dropped Byron off at his castle, and Dirk and I were back at Bilford's Bread, Brew, & Bedding by sunrise. Eve greeted us at the door with hugs!

"Good morning, Sunshine," I said, hugging her tight.

"Miss us?" Dirk asked, messing up her neatly brushed hair.

"No," she answered with a big smile, hugging him too.

"She didn't cause any trouble for you, did she?" I asked Bilford while he was taking bread out of a stone oven behind the counter.

"Not a bit," he answered. "She's a darling of a girl."

"I haven't even been outside," she whispered to us.

I bent over and asked her in a low tone, "Has he kept you from leaving?" I noticed she looked paler than usual, and the veins in her face and hands looked more pronounced.

"No," she answered bashfully. "He told me stories about terrible monsters, so I was too scared to go out alone."

"It's okay," I told her. "Dirk, will you take her out for a little while? Wear your cloaks and keep to the shadows. Don't be gone long."

With a nod, Dirk took her out for a drink, and I sat at one of the tables to put my wounded leg up for a moment. No one else was in the bar this early in the morning, so I had time to relax. At least, I thought I did.

"That's quite a burn you have their," Bilford commented. "A lesser man wouldn't be able to walk, much less sit calmly in my bar."

He knows! I glared at him, and he glared right back with unwavering eyes. The jolly, old barkeep that

I knew was gone. Now, I faced the aged vampire hunter.

I planted both feet on the floor and began to stand when a dagger hit me in the chest! I looked down to see it was buried all the way to the hilt, into my heart! Another dagger was thrown at me, but I moved out of its path. I leaped across the room toward the old vampire hunter, calling an ethereal shield to my hand! I landed on the bar, raising the shield just in time to block another attack! He had swung a short sword, and it would have taken my head off had I not blocked it. The blade of his sword banged hard against my shield, causing him to drop it. I struck him with the shield and grabbed him by the throat, lifting him off the floor.

"You're quick, old man," I snarled.

He held onto my wrist, trying to relieve some of the weight put on his neck, but he couldn't speak. Only a gurgling sound came from his mouth. I let go of my shield and took his belt of knives away from him.

"I like you, Bilford. That's why I'm not going to kill you." I released my grip from his neck, and he fell to the floor, coughing.

I pulled the dagger from my chest. I grunted, for it was quite painful, sending a tingling sensation throughout my entire body. I saw him reach for the sword that he had dropped. "No. No," I said with a smile, pushing it away with my power.

With a flick of his wrist, he threw another dagger at me while I was distracted by his sword! I raised a hand up to shield my face, but I didn't have time to use my power. The dagger pierced my hand! He had been keeping it hidden in his wooden leg.

"You truly are a formidable vampire hunter," I congratulated him, pulling the dagger from my hand.

"I've been around the undead enough to see through your disguises," he said, getting his wooden leg turned around, so he could stand up.

I got down from the bar to help the old man. I had forgotten about his missing leg. "I'm sorry," I apologized.

With a confused look on his face, he asked, "You're sorry? Why?"

I took his belt of knives with me, so he couldn't get hold of them again and picked up his sword, sheathing it. I limped back around the counter to retrieve a dagger from the wall before customers began coming in. "I'm sorry because my leg will heal back to normal, but yours will never grow back. That is, if you never accept eternal life."

"You asking if I'd become a bloodsucker like you? Forget it," he answered quickly. "You turned that innocent little girl, didn't you?"

Slamming the belt on his counter, I answered, "I saved her . . . from being killed by her own people! She was being sacrificed to their god, and I couldn't let that happen! I didn't let it happen."

"I can think of worse ways to die," he stated, pouring himself a drink and downing it quickly only to pour another. "I'd rather die a hero to my people than alone as a monster."

"But she is so young," I argued to explain my actions.

"We all die, son," he said calmly, "even vampires. Forever isn't as long as you may think. Even the world won't last forever. Wandering for centuries while everyone else dies, and watching the world around you fall to ruin doesn't appeal to me."

"The world will not fall to ruin; I will save it."

Bilford laughed at my confidence. "I'm afraid the world is too big for you, my friend, and has already fallen too far into decay."

"I killed the Sea Giants," I boasted.

"Only one terrible race of many," he fired back effortlessly.

"I also killed the strigoi."

"HA! It is the necromancer that must be killed."

I suddenly realized he was right. Byron created them and could make all he wanted. Without the dragons ruling, who's to say he wouldn't try to take control again? I could find myself going to war against him someday.

"I need his help," I finally said to Bilford, "but if you, a mortal, can see that I'm really a vampire then surely he can. That means I need to cover my tracks better . . . starting with you."

I reached out, gripping him with my telekinesis while I walked around the counter. I saw fear in his eyes.

"I told you that I wasn't going to kill you, and I meant it," I said, putting his belt back under the counter. "However, I do need to alter your thoughts a bit," I added with a grin.

I took his arm and sank my teeth in. I drank slowly, invading his mind to remove the knowledge that my companions and I were vampires. I then put his mind to sleep and sat him gently on the floor behind the bar. I bit my finger and rubbed the blood on the bite mark to heal the wound before returning to my chair.

I took a deep breath and exhaled my frustration. I could feel the dark blood repairing my heart and closing the flesh. I looked at my hand and saw that it was also healing quickly. The damage to my leg was much more extensive, so it would take several days to heal. I used my new spell to change my clothes so that my wounded leg wasn't visible.

I heard Bilford grumbling from where I left him on the floor, behind the bar.

"Bilford, you okay?" I asked, running around the bar to help him stand.

"Thank you, sir Magnus. What happened?"

"You collapsed. Are you okay? It looks like you hit your head." He will probably have a black eye from where I hit him with my shield.

"AH, it's this damned leg," he cursed. "It gives way with me sometimes."

"You need to be more careful," I said just as his first customer of the day came in for some freshly baked bread.

I stepped out from behind the bar, so he could run his business.

"Good morning, Lou," he greeted the man, rubbing his face.

Dirk and Eve were back well before lunch. We went to our room, so I could tell them what happened while they were gone. I explained to them that we needed to be more careful when dealing with others because we don't know how they'll react to us.

"What about Byron?" Dirk asked.

"I'm trying to convince him that I'm a dragon that takes human form, but I can't read his thoughts to see if it's working. I can't see how much he actually knows or suspects. What I do know is that Byron is very powerful, so we should be cautious."

CHAPTER XIII

THE STORM GIANTS

We stayed at Bilford's Bread, Brew, & Bedding for several days while my leg healed. I even let Eve drink human blood while I was there to watch over her. I taught her and Dirk how to search people's thoughts and manipulate memories.

I stood up from the table where I had been sitting in the barroom with my children. The place was full that evening. I told Dirk I was going to take a walk in the forest to clear my head before I decide our next plan of action.

Eve followed me to the door. "Can I go with you?" she asked with a bit of excitement.

"I'm going to meditate, and I have to be alone to do it."

"Oh, okay," she said disappointedly.

I kissed her on the forehead, bringing a smile

back to her face. "I need you to stay here and take care of your brother."

"Oh, I'll take care of him," she said, turning to look at him sitting at the table, punching her fist into her hand.

"HAHAA!" I laughed at her. "Go on. Jump on him."

She ran through the crowded bar and playfully jumped on Dirk, punching him in the side. Dirk did nothing but laugh as his chair tipped over, and they fell in the barroom floor.

"All right now," Bilford spoke up from behind the bar, chuckling. "No bar fights."

"I'll be back soon," I spoke out over the laughing patrons. I pulled the hood of my cloak up and stepped out into the afternoon sun.

I walked into the forest and spoke out to the evening sky, "We did it. Vistilia, we did it." I was suddenly so overwhelmed with relief that tears filled my eyes. "With the power you bestowed upon me, I have avenged our family's death and reclaimed our homeland. Wherever you are," I said to the coming stars, "I miss you dearly and wish you were here with me now." Even after all she's done, I still loved her.

I pulled my hood back and sat down on a fallen tree. I then closed my eyes so that I may catch a glimpse of the future that will soon be upon me. I saw Eve in Ashwood. I saw Assim flying over a snowy forest. He wasn't helping the Storm Giants expand their territory; he was fighting against them to defend Woodland Elves. I also saw a greater army of giants than that on Crete and the sun rising before the battle is over. The visions were vague, but I felt confident that we will once again prevail.

I returned to find Eve and Dirk sitting outside of Bilford's bar.

"So what did you see?" Eve asked eagerly, running up to me in the street.

"We have more giants to fight."

"So I get to go this time?"

"I'm afraid not, Sunshine," I answered, putting my arm around her shoulder while we walked to Dirk. "You'll be staying with the elves. Your brother and I have a bright, sunny day ahead of us."

"But the sun burns," Dirk uttered with an expression of dread.

"Well, it's been nice knowing you," Eve joked, patting him on the arm.

"HA! I'd rather spend a day in the sun than a minute with elves," he commented.

With no mortals around to see, I transformed into a dragon right there in the center of town. I picked up my children and carried them to the Dark Hills where the Dark Elven city of Ashwood lay within a dormant volcano. Returning to human form, the three of us dropped to the forest floor.

Torvin and the other elf hunters were there as usual to greet us, "Welcome back, my lord."

"Thank you. Our stay will be short, for we have business in the north. We are here to give Eve a place to stay while Dirk and I are gone."

"She's welcome to stay in Ambros' hut," Torvin told us. "I don't think he'll be coming back to it."

"What? Ambros isn't here?" Eve asked me, noticeably disappointed.

"I'm sorry, Sunshine," I said to her, rubbing her

shoulder.

We followed Torvin to the obsidian entrance of the city. He placed his hand on it and concentrated for a moment. "This door can only be activated by Dark Elves, but now that you are our guardian," he said to me, "place your hand on the stone, and you will be given access to Ashwood."

I did as he said, and the large, obsidian elves moved for us to enter.

Thanking him, we passed through the cave to the city. It felt good to be back. The few elves that were out at this early hour greeted us with smiles and bows.

We arrived at Ambrosius' old home and saw that most everything was still where we remembered it.

"Ambros must have loaded down his dead goat with what little it could carry and never made a return trip," Dirk commented.

"All I can tell is missing are some of Ambrosius' scrolls, a few elixirs, and the obsidian weapons that were on the table," I said aloud as I checked the rooms.

"What should we do with all these things?" Dirk asked from an adjacent room.

I walked over to see him slipping his hand into a dark gauntlet with a blue obsidian gem set in the palm. "Hmm," I thought for a moment. "Once we've taken care of the giants, we should find a safe place to store these things and other artifacts that we may come across."

Dirk removed the gauntlet and placed it back in the box that he found it in.

I saw Eve standing in the doorway of Ambros' bedroom. She stood quietly, touching his necklace that she still wore.

I put my arm around her shoulder to comfort her. "His father sent him on a different path," I told her. "I'm sure it's for the best."

"But who will keep me company while you're gone?" she asked, looking up at me.

"There must be plenty of children here your age to play with."

She walked into the room and picked up a small skeleton doll from the boy's bed. "None quite like him," she said with a smile.

Laughing, I said, "You're probably right on that."

I stepped outside where Dirk was sitting on the porch with his eyes shut and his feet propped up on the railing. "So we're going to slay more giants? What's the plan?" he asked me.

I took a seat next to him and looked out at the city lights that burned like stars in the night. Outside of Ashwood, the morning sun should be rising about now, but it would be dark here for a few more hours.

"The council," I began, "is gathering their forces to initiate world war."

"World war," he repeated in shock, sitting up in his chair. "By the gods."

"It was the Dragon Council that set giants loose against us," I explained. "They want the world for themselves."

Dirk shook his head. "I'm sure it won't take them long to find out that they are missing their giants," he stressed. "What are we going to do?"

"We will kill the Storm Giants of the north the same as we did the Sea Giants of Crete," I answered. "I will then look into the future for our next step."

Dirk stood from his chair. "If you see an end to our future, let me know." He jumped over the porch railing and dropped far below to the ground.

I quickly stood up to look over the railing. "Where are you going?"

"I'm going out for a drink," he answered before disappearing into the city.

A few minutes later, Eve came outside and took Dirk's chair beside me. "When do you plan to leave?"

"At sunset," I answered, holding her little hand.

I heard her breathe a sigh of sadness. "But you saved your land. Why can't we just stay here and be happy?" she implored.

"We could stay here, but the world around us would be destroyed. Yes, I did what I set out to do: I reclaimed my homeland, but now I see that it's much bigger than that. I believe I am the only person that can make a difference, and if I don't stand up and do something, we will lose everything."

"I wish Vistilia were here," she said sadly.

"I know you do but…," I began to say, but she got up and ran into the house. "Eve." I followed her inside.

"Please, come back!" she yelled with crimson tears streaming down her face. "Mommy, come back!" she pleaded.

I held her in my arms while she wept for Vistilia to return.

"You would stay if she was here. We would be together, a family. Can't she hear me? Why won't she come back? Doesn't she miss us? Doesn't she love me?"

"Oh sweetheart, she does love you, just as I love you," I answered, choked up from my own tears, "but I don't know why she doesn't come back to us."

"I want to lie down," she said to me, so I kissed her forehead and let her go to Ambros' room.

I sat outside until Dirk returned. When it was time for us to leave, we said our goodbyes to Eve.

"See you soon, sister," Dirk said, giving her a hug. "Don't stink up the place while we're gone," he joked.

She chuckled and responded with, "I'm going to fill this place up with dead goats just for you, brother."

Dirk laughed. "I'd like to see you carry all those rotten animals up here. You get sick from just looking at them. I can't imagine you holding them."

They both laughed at the thought.

I bent down to give her a hug. "Behave yourself while we're gone. Okay?"

"I will," she answered.

I kissed her on the cheek. "I love you, Evelyn, my little sunshine."

She returned the kiss, saying, "I love you too, Pop."

"I think you spent far too much time with Ambros," I laughed. "He was a bad influence on you."

"Somewhere written on one of these scrolls may be the skill to breathe life into dead animals," Dirk mentioned, looking around at what was left.

"Yuck!" Eve expressed. "I'm not doing that. I'm not breathing into a dead animal's mouth. That's gross."

We all laughed again, and I hugged her once more before Dirk and I left Ashwood to pick up Byron.

When we reached the necromancer's castle, Dirk ran to the hole that led to the throne room. "Byron," he called down to him, "we have more giants to slay."

We heard the centurions begin talking amongst themselves.

"Giants! They're big!" we discerned one of them say.

"And frightening," another added.

"Frighteningly giant!"

"We need them on our side," we heard another speak out, and then they all began agreeing with him.

Moments later, they all became quiet, and Byron rose forth from his den, wielding the staff that I had bestowed him.

"Good evening, gentlemen," he greeted us.

"Let's hope so, king," I said to him.

I picked them up and flew north against bitter winds.

"WOO!" Dirk blew. "Do you mind loaning me some furs?" he yelled to me over the strong winds and snow.

I took a moment to concentrate on changing Dirk's clothing to better suit the climate change. He was soon wearing thick furs to better withstand the cold.

"What about you?" I asked Byron. "Do you need warmer clothes?"

"None for me, thank you. I have my own magic to keep me warm."

"Very well," I laughed.

As we continued flying north, I told them, "The giants are attacking an elven city that blocks passage to the more populated regions of the south. We will be siding with the elves, so we can defeat the giants as quickly as possible."

"Great, more elves," Dirk commented.

Burning trees and the clashing sounds of battle

told us we had reached our destination. We landed on an icy beach at the edge of a snow-covered city, away from the fighting.

The elves' huts were built around the trunks of trees like many of the huts in Ashwood. These, however, were constructed of stone and mud, so they could only be built on the ground. It looked like it was once a nice, peaceful city but now, their homes were damaged, trees were broken, and bodies of both elves and giants stained the snow with death.

"Do your thing," I told Byron, "but don't disturb the elves because we don't want to seem inconsiderate."

He reached into a pouch hanging from his belt and sprinkled a small amount of dust in the wounds of a fallen giant. He then took a drink of some sort of liquid from a bladder that he also had tied on his belt and spat it in the giant's face. It took only moments for the magic to take effect. We began to hear gurgling moans come from the dead giant's tusk filled mouth, and its enormous hands clawed at the world around it.

Taking a closer look at the monster as it slowly climbed to its feet, I saw that its black eyes reflected Byron's Dark Elven face. The falling snow seemed to distract it, but once we had three other zombie giants ready for war, Byron gave them a mental command to charge into battle where there's plenty of their kin to gorge themselves upon.

Both Dirk and I summoned an ethereal short spear and shield before following our undead troops through the battered city into war. We reached a clearing where huts were trampled and large trees had been pushed over. The elves were fighting hard but were losing against the mighty giants. Their swords seemed like knives against such hulking monsters, and it took many well placed arrows to bring one down.

The Woodland Elves wore many layers of fur to stay warm here in these cold lands. They also wore elk antlers on their shoulders for protection in battle.

Terror filled the elves when they saw mortally wounded giants return to the battlefield but cheered when they attacked their own kind! That terror then filled the giants, for they knew not how to react to their fallen comrades turning their teeth on them.

I found out the hard way that a shield was nearly worthless when defending against a massive war hammer with the strength of a Storm Giant behind it. The beast laughed when he swung with enough force to knock me over a hundred feet!

After shaking off the stars I saw twinkling around my head, I charged toward my enemy empty handed. The 20' tall giant readied his hammer made of ice, but it was I who surprised him this time. Just before reaching him, I transformed into a dragon and tail whipped him so hard that he exploded!

I turned towards a group of giants and breathed fire on them, but it had no effect on them, just like the Storm Giant I fought in Crete. They ran to attack me with their axes and hammers of ice, but I escaped them by flying away from the battlefield.

One of the elves spotted me and turned into a dragon to join me in the air. It was Assim.

"Magnus, I am so glad to see you," he said to me, high above the war torn forest. "But I am confused why you're helping me fight against the giants when we were both ordered to aid them in their march south from the Cold Mountains."

"I too joined the council believing I could make a difference in the world, but I don't agree with its direction," I told him truthfully.

"Well, I'm glad you're here, friend," he told me. "We definitely need all the help we can get. Now let's go win this war!"

I followed him into a dive to the forest clearing below where we continued our fight against the Storm Giants.

Dirk protected Byron while he brought the dead giants back to fight for us. Dirk also found that a shield wasn't helpful in this fight and decided to use a long handled ethereal axe.

Byron tried to strike a giant with a bolt of lightning from his magical staff, but the monster seemed shielded from it as well. After two zombie giants brought the hulking beast down, Byron had one of them carry him across the battlefield to speak to me.

"There must be a shaman somewhere nearby that is protecting these giants from elemental attacks," he yelled at me over the chaos.

I sent a telepathic message to Dirk. He and Assim were holding the clearing with a band of elves. *"Fall back to my location as soon as possible."*

"We must find this shaman if we are to defeat the Storm Giants," I told Byron.

Dirk met with us where I told him the plan. "The three of us must scout ahead in search of a shaman that is protecting our enemies with elemental resistances. If we can eliminate him, Assim and I will then be able to burn them."

"How are we going to find this shaman?" Dirk asked.

Looking to Byron, he answered, "We should be able to spot him from the sky."

I took us up and circled around the elven city. The winds were cold and thick with snow, but my enhanced vision cut through to see all the warm bodies below. I could spot the zombies movements, but they didn't put off any heat for me to see easily.

By following the direction from which the giants were charging to war, I was able to locate a large bonfire burning blue fire. Three Storm Giants chanted by the firelight.

"There they are," Byron pointed out.

"Call your zombies, because this is about to get rough."

I released my warriors from high in the air and dove in behind them. Snow pelted me in the face as I dropped from the sky. While we were falling, I saw Dirk ready a long, ethereal spear, and a spike of ice formed on the end of Byron's magical staff.

Just before Dirk speared one of the giant shamans, it turned, firing a bolt of lightning from its hand! It hit Dirk, arced to Byron, but passed by me. Both Dirk and Byron fell hard to the ground, stunned by the attack. I dropped right on their bonfire. The giants shielded their faces from the cinders that stirred in my wake.

I released a powerful yell and breathed fire on them, but like the others, they were unharmed by it. I swung my long, crimson tail, knocking one giant into another.

The remaining giant punched me in the face with a massive, ice-coated fist. I staggered, and the monster grabbed the black horns of my head. It fought to break my neck, but Dirk leaped up from behind, plunging a spear of ethereal energy through the giant's chest!

The snow stopped falling and the clouds began to thin. Sunrise was approaching! Perhaps it wasn't a coincidence that the storm lifted just as Dirk killed that giant.

I returned to human form, but before I could create a weapon, one of the giants charged at us with a hammer created of ice. It knocked both me and Dirk into the forest.

The giant turned to attack Byron, but the necromancer fired a bolt of lightning from his staff. It didn't harm the giant but caused its hammer to explode into bits of ice.

Without transforming fully into a dragon, I used leathery wings to climb into the air. As Dirk ran back into battle to help Byron, I dove toward the giant with an ethereal spear. The giant magically created another ice hammer, but just before swinging it against Dirk, I buried my spear deep into its shoulder! It then turned its attention to me. I started to fly away from him, but it struck me with the hammer, knocking me out of the air. Before the giant could hit me again, Byron pierced it with several spikes of ice, and the giant fell to the snow-covered ground.

We still had one shaman remaining, and the morning sun was beginning to break through the forest to burn me and Dirk to ash! Remembering the first shaman that Dirk killed, I quickly scrambled over to drink its blood and search its mind for the ability to create storms. I bit into the beast's neck. Its thick blood oozed into my mouth, and I followed its flow to the brain for answers.

"Watch out!" I heard Dirk yell.

Looking from my meal, I saw the last giant charge through both Dirk and Byron, easily knocking them away. The giant raised his massive fists and arctic winds swirled around them, taking the form of a large war axe! I tried to telekinetically push him back, but the giant was too powerful to hold back. I raised my arm to create a shield when Byron's zombie giants stormed out of the forest to attack the remaining shaman. He tried to defend himself but was quickly overpowered and brought down.

I could feel the morning sun approaching but continued to search for the Storm Giant's power. I knew it was here, buried in its dying mind, but would I reach it in time? Would I reach the knowledge before it faded, or would I have to hide among the trees until nightfall, revealing to Byron that sunlight is both mine and Dirk's weakness?

From the giant's fading memories, I saw that the Storm Giants were once known as the Frost Giants. Their increasing power over the weather slowly earned them the new name. And there it was, the knowledge I was looking for! It was the power to send moisture into the sky to form clouds and create precipitation!

I released my bite from the giant and turned my gaze to the sky where the sun's morning light was beginning to creep over me. Focusing my thoughts on what I must do, clouds began to form and fill the sky to block out the light!

Climbing to my feet, I saw the last shaman being consumed by the zombie giants.

"Search their minds for anything useful," I told Dirk. "I'm returning to the city to kill off the remaining

Storm Giants."

I transformed into a dragon and flew back to where Assim and the Woodland Elves were still fighting the Storm Giant warriors. With my new found power, I was finally free to move about during the day! I was no longer hindered by the sun, and it felt good.

I dove along a charging line of giants, breathing fire across them. Their resistance to fire didn't hold this time, and they were burned to a crisp. Cheers from the elves rang out, for victory was soon at hand! Assim joined me in the sky to kill every last giant as they turned to flee into the forest.

Once the Storm Giants were defeated, we flew back to the city where we were greeted by the surviving Woodland Elves and their chieftain. Dirk and Byron had already returned. I took human form while Assim took the form of an elf.

The proud, elven chieftain approached to speak to us on behalf of his people.

"I am Magnus the Red Dragon Lord," I told him. "This is Assim the Yellow Dragon Lord, and my companions, Byron and Dirk."

"I am Garren, chieftain here. We are pleased to meet you, but we are already quite familiar with Lord Assim; he has been our city guardian for many years," the elf informed me. "From the bottom of our hearts, we cannot thank you enough. You have proven to us yet again that the majestic dragons of the World Council will always come to our aid when we need it most. We are also very grateful for your help, cousin," he said to Byron, unaware that he was only wearing the body of a Dark Elf. "Your service here today rekindles our hope that the three elven races can set aside our past differences, and reforge our kinship."

Byron bowed to the elf chieftain but said not a word, fearing any questions he asked would raise suspicion that he was not who he appeared to be.

"Our broken forest will return, but you have vanquished the Storm Giants forever," Garren said to us. "And for that, we thank you."

Garren bowed, followed by his people.

"I don't know how you did it, but I'm glad you did," Assim whispered to me.

We helped the elves gather the dead and stacked wood to lay the bodies on. That's when I heard the elf chieftain speak of an afterlife.

"When someone dies," he began to explain, "their body must be burned to release the spirit, so it may fly to the Sun."

"Do giants go there too?" I asked, looking at the separate pile of bodies that was to be burned.

"They do," he answered with a smile. "Every living thing will one day exist together in harmony within the divine light of the Sun."

It sounded like just another version of the afterlife that I had heard all my life. These poor, misguided fools, I thought.

"We may have been enemies in this world, but we will be friends in the next," the chieftain preached as he lit fires with a torch.

"Thank you for your enlightening message," I said, turning to walk away with Assim.

"What about the Sea Giants of the south?" Assim asked as we walked together through the battered city. "Have you already met with them?"

"They've been taken care of," I answered coldly.

"I take it you killed them. Are we going to attack the Fire Giants? What are we going to do about the council when they find out what we've done?"

"I need time to meditate," I told him.

"Very well," he answered. "I will help the elves until you return."

Walking to the edge of the city, I found a quiet place to sit on the snow-covered beach. Waves stood still on a frozen ocean that bridged this northern region to the southern where the Storm Giants planned to invade.

I closed my eyes, and I saw a mountainous desert. A system of caves tunneled deep within the mountains was home to the last race of Giants. They were shorter than the Sea Giants but were more fiendish in appearance. Their skin was red as blood, and their hair was a black mane around black horns. I saw Assim carrying Byron. I also saw water, lots of water. The vision ended, leaving me confused about water in the desert.

I wonder what these visions will show after the Fire Giants are defeated. Will I be returning to attack the Woodland Elves, or will I have to kill every member of the World Council so I become the new ruler? I need to know what races exist before I set my plan into motion. I'm sure there's more than what I've seen and what the council has mentioned. While I'm here, perhaps I can prepare the elves for their extermination.

I walked back through the war torn city to where everyone was gathered, paying their respects to the dead. I heard the elf chieftain chanting loudly over the burning fires.

"…And may your spirits rejoice in the splendor

of the Sun!" Garren shouted, raising his arms to the cloudy sky. His people all stood around the many funeral pyres, holding torches.

I stood next to him and waited patiently until he acknowledged my presence. Dirk, Byron, and Assim were sitting on a fallen tree not far away and came over to listen to what I had to say.

"Yes, Lord Magnus. How may I assist you?" Garren asked courteously.

"What caused the elves to part ways?" I asked, deeply curious.

The wind began picking up, so Garren motioned for us to follow him to a hut that wasn't completely destroyed. Inside, he started a fire in the fire pit, and we all sat on the dirt floor around it to hear his story.

"Ages ago, before the first humans," he began, looking at me and the form I took, "there were the Elves. They weren't Woodland Elves. They weren't Dark Elves. They weren't Light Elves. They were simply Elves. Before the dragons came, they worshipped the great phoenixes, powerful fire spirits that inhabited the body of large, beautiful birds." Raising his arms, the flames of the fire rose up like a bird taking flight!

"The phoenixes were believed to have brought the seeds of life to this planet," he continued. "Shedding their physical forms, all but one left our world. The last phoenix, known as Arethil, stayed to transform the earth into a warm, lush paradise for life to flourish. That all changed when the dragons rose from the deepest depths of the earth." He raised his arms this time, and a dragon took shape from the firelight.

The way he told his story reminded me a lot of how Ambrosius told me of the Draconian Wars.

"Were the dragons already here before the phoenixes arrived?" Assim asked.

"We believe they formed within the earth sometime after the planet was seeded with life. It was said that the earth itself cracked, giving birth to the mighty serpents. The lands split and began drifting apart. Cold winds began blowing from the north and slowly crept across the lands to wither all life."

Snow blew in through the broken ceiling to give us all a sudden chill. Dirk stoked the fire with a few pieces of wood from a nearby stack.

With the fire burning hot again, he continued with his tale. "Where the phoenix Arethil instilled peace among the world's inhabitants, the dragons took slaves and incited chaos. They transformed the world, bringing war and leaving death. They desired to be worshiped as gods over all life, and many fought their own kind for dominancy as supreme ruler. A terrible serpent named Shadowrath rose to become just that, King of Dragons. He was unlike any dragon this world has ever seen."

The flames of the fire pit lowered, and the rising smoke and cinders took the shape of a terrifying dragon.

"With the Great Winter approaching, Arethil remained a source of light for the elves as the world closed in around them. The great phoenix held off Shadowrath's army so that the elves could escape and sacrificed herself to destroy the terrible dragon. The elves parted ways and never truly reconnected. To find refuge from the cold, some went deep below ground. Another group journeyed south, holding onto hope of finding a warmer climate. The remaining elves learned to hunt and build shelters to survive the Great Winter."

"They became the three races of elves," Assim

spoke.

"Yes," Garren nodded. "We, the Woodland Elves, are the descendants of those who faced the Great Winter." Looking at Byron, he said, "Those that went underground became the Dark Elves. And those who ventured south became known as the Light Elves."

I clearly remembered Ambrosius telling me that he himself led his people into that volcano during the Draconian Wars and yet, here, Garren is telling me that it happened before humans walked the earth! That seemed like an impossibly long time ago!

"Where are the Light Elves now?" Assim inquired. "They too could be in danger."

"Sometime after the Great Winter, Woodland Elves came into contact with them. They were described as enchantingly beautiful and hungry for knowledge. They moved often, but their village was always called Lylandria, which currently lies west of here."

"If the great phoenixes were fire spirits, what happened to Arethil after her sacrifice?" Byron asked, intrigued by the tale.

"Now that, cousin, remains a mystery," Garren answered. "Some say her spirit flew to the Sun where she continues to watch over us. Others say her remains were locked away before she could separate from her body. Then there are those who say the entire story is a fairy tale."

"And what do you believe," I asked him.

Garren laughed. "Take heed of a fairy's tale, for their words carry much weight. But just look around you," he said, raising his hands. "Winter is still upon us, and darkness still comes. Arethil's light does not shine down upon us, so we continue to live as we have for generations: by surviving." He paused for a moment, staring at the burning fire. "We did not wish harm upon the giants, but they brought the war to us with plans to kill many more." Garren broke down into tears.

"Why don't you send word to your kin to build a grand city?" I asked. "That way, you will be stronger in number, and we can better protect you from future attacks."

"That is an excellent idea," Garren said, wiping his face. "Perhaps we can once again bring our beloved cousins together and restore peace to our race," he added, looking at Byron.

"Once we take care of another threat to the southeast, we will return to help with planning and construction," I told him, standing to leave. "We will return as soon as our task is complete."

"Thank you, Lord Magnus," the elf chieftain said. "Thank you all, and may you have a safe journey."

My companions and I stepped out into the bitter cold and walked to the far end of the clearing, so we could take flight without disrupting the elves' ceremony. As they watched their fallen brethren burn on funeral pyres, they wished them farewell, repeating Garren's words, "May your spirits rejoice in the splendor of the Sun."

I heard Dirk say under his breath, "Glad to get away from all this elf shit for a while."

Assim turned to him and asked, "You don't share their beliefs?"

"No, absolutely not," Dirk answered bluntly. "I believed that I would be allowed into Paradise—until I died."

"You mean, you were denied entry?" Assim

asked in disbelief.

"I mean, there was no Paradise. There was nothing. I wanted to see my wife and son again, if only for a moment, but where are they? They're dead! They're gone, forever."

Byron spoke up to share his thoughts. "How can you believe we would be awarded eternal life in Paradise after living a pathetic existence in this world? There is no Paradise unless we create it for ourselves."

"That's what the council is planning to do," Assim exclaimed. "Their plan is to create their own paradise."

Byron laughed. "Those hotheaded lizards will continue to fight for supremacy until they destroy everything. No offense," he said, suddenly remembering that Assim could incinerate him with a single breath.

"There's no need to apologize," Assim told him genuinely. "You're entitled to your opinion. In fact, I'm interested in hearing it. If I were to become head of the World Council, I would work hard to maintain the peace, so my children wouldn't have to grow up in such chaos."

"I hate to interrupt this discussion, but we need to be heading on to our next objective," I announced.

"Yes, we certainly do," Assim agreed, "before the council finds out what we're doing."

"War for peace," Byron said, shaking his head. "Dragons just don't get it."

"Then why is it that you fight?" Assim asked him after taking his true form.

"I want to change the world for the better, not for the worse. I can't do that with dragons making a mess of things."

CHAPTER XIV

THE FIRE GIANTS

To the desert east of the Mediterranean, Assim and I flew. He and Byron wanted to talk more during the flight, so they traveled together. We had left the elves midafternoon, so night had fallen before we reached the land of the Fire Giants. While passing over the mountains, Dirk spotted two, axe wielding giants guarding a large cave.

"If they too have night vision, they've no doubt spotted us as well," he mentioned.

"Then how about we drop in on them?" I suggested.

"Let's take them out."

With that, I immediately took human form so that I was harder to spot from the ground. Dirk and I fell from the sky, straight towards the two guards. As we drew closer, we could tell they were looking up, but it was Assim's movements that they were following. They did not see us falling through the darkness.

Dirk fired a bolt of magical energy to strike one of the hulking beasts in the head. He used telekinesis to slow his descent.

Just before impact with the other guard, I brought out my wings and summoned a long ethereal sword to cleave my enemy in two from shoulder to waist. I then landed quietly on the sand.

Staring into the mouth of the cave, Dirk whispered, "So what's the plan?"

An idea formed, and I spoke to Byron's mind with a silent voice. *"Have Assim take you to the shore; I need you to bring water, lots of water."*

"Yes, Lord Magnus."

Assim turned and flew back toward the ocean.

I looked over the two giants, and they were every bit as fiendish as they were in my visions. They had thick, red leathery hides and tusks protruding from angry lips. They wore human skulls as jewelry and dragon scales as light armor.

"We need to get going," I said aloud to remind myself.

We quietly entered the large cavern. The cave was illuminated by fire burning in bowls. Small, black stones, not wood, fueled these fires.

We walked for several minutes before we caught sound of something farther ahead of us. Dirk placed his ear to the cavern floor.

"They are passing through a cave intersection not far ahead of us," he silently informed me.

We cautiously moved on to find about two dozen Fire Giants leading camels down an intersecting tunnel. The camels pulled wooden cages filled with humans that the giants had recently captured.

"*How can we save these people?*" Dirk asked telepathically.

"*We won't be able to,*" I answered sadly, "*but we can save others from being taken. Come on. I want to see what they're doing down here in the mountains.*"

We followed the giants deep into the core of the mountain. While they lumbered down the tunnel, they spoke to one another in an indiscernible language and laughed about whatever they were talking about. I looked into their thoughts and saw visions of them attacking a village to the south. They killed all who stood against them and took the others captive.

Dirk grabbed my arm to stop me. Ahead of us, the giants reached another intersecting tunnel where they stopped to speak with other giants. The spear-wielding giants looked over the people that they had captured and grunted their approval of their catch.

"*If they come this way, they'll see us and alert every giant in this mountain of our presence,*" Dirk expressed his concern.

The tunnel was clear of anything that we could easily hide behind, and I couldn't use my dragon wings because the wind and sound from them would give us away. My only other option was to try lifting us with my thoughts.

"*Remain still,*" I told Dirk as I concentrated on lifting us. Slowly, we began floating to the high ceiling of the cavern.

"*It's working!*" I heard Dirk's mind say excitedly.

The giants that we were following continued on

their way down the tunnel. The others came walking in our direction. I held us aloft about twelve feet above them. I could feel Dirk's anxiety as three Fire Giants passed beneath us. Once they disappeared into the darkness, I carefully lowered us to the dirt floor and followed the tracks left by the camel carts.

We tracked them to a vast cavern where two hundred or more giants were gathered. The arrival of the camel carts and their bounty brought cheers from their race.

The cavern had many tunnels leading into it from various heights. One particularly large tunnel was lined with painted skulls and had a stone platform built out from it with strange symbols carved into it. Some of the skulls were unmistakably human, but I was unfamiliar with the others.

The camel carts were positioned in front of the platform and the cages opened. There were at least thirty human prisoners that had to be prodded out of their cages; they didn't seem too eager to be released into a horde of sinister giants. Once the frightened captives were out and the cages moved, the giants began chanting, "SMITE! SMITE! SMITE! SMITE! SMITE! SMITE!"

Dirk and I remained hidden to see what was about to happen. The chanting grew to a thundering roar, and just when we thought the very mountain would come crashing down to quiet the sound, an enormous Blue Dragon stormed out of the decorated tunnel! It held its head high, reveling in the roars of its followers. The prisoners covered their ears from the sound and cried at the sight of the dragon.

The Blue Dragon spoke in the language of the

giants, and its booming voice brought them to silence. I reached out to its mind and was able to read its thoughts as it spoke.

The group of Fire Giants that Dirk and I had followed here were the last to arrive. The dragon had divided its force to conquer the surrounding human settlements and now planned to push south, deeper into the Arab region, and west through the southern Mediterranean countries.

I also found that Smite was the dragon's name, and he will take a seat on the World Council once his army completes their campaign. He wants to propose building another Council Palace in this part of the world where he could lead his own council of dragons.

A small group of prisoners mustered up the courage to make a run for it! They ran towards the cave where Dirk and I were crouched. Sparks crackled along the great dragon's teeth, and a bolt of lightning arced from person to person. They exploded into clouds of ash! Cheers from the giants and cries from the remaining prisoners once again filled the immense cavern.

"*I think it's time we break up this party,*" I told Dirk, stepping out to reveal our presence. The cavern fell dead silent as all eyes fell on me and Dirk.

"Who is this pathetic creature with the audacity to stand before the mighty Smite?" the great dragon questioned, bringing a laugh from his army. Torch light glistened off his blue scales, making them look like precious sapphires.

Dirk stepped forward to introduce me. "May I present, Magnus the Red Dragon Lord of the World Council."

The cavern fell silent again. Smite bowed his head from his platform high above us, and the Fire Giants all kneeled before me. Even the human prisoners were quiet while they huddled together with no hope of escaping.

"Forgive me, my lord," Smite apologized for his rudeness. "What does the council wish of its most loyal servant?"

"The council requests that you cease your campaign to control the Arab region," I announced. "The elves of the north have begun construction of a grand city where they will gather their race. That is where the World Council will direct its attention for the foreseeable future."

"My lord, the humans are expanding at an ever-increasing rate," Smite explained. "Our strength outmatches their numbers now, but if we delay the assault, we will be forfeiting our advantage."

"I understand that, but the council has other plans for the humans," I told him. Sensing his doubt in calling off the attack, I felt I should divert his thoughts. "You have a better view of things here on the front lines," I began. "Perhaps you can bring your view of the situation to Lord Grimlash's attention when you return to the World Council Palace with me."

"*Um, Magnus?*" I heard Dirk say telepathically from behind me.

"Yes," Smite answered. "I most certainly will. Even if we have to divide our force between the elves and the humans, we cannot afford to abandon the lands we've already cleared."

"*Magnus?*" Dirk called again.

"That sounds like an acceptable compromise," I

told Smite.

"Magnus!" Dirk finally said aloud.

I turned my head to see Dirk standing behind me, holding a sword toward the dark tunnel. Three Fire Giants charged through him wielding flaming axes! I raised my left hand to arm myself with a magical weapon, but one of the monstrous beasts swung his axe, cleaving my arm at the elbow! His fire axe instantly cauterized the wound. He then kicked me into Smite's stone platform.

The giant charged at me again, holding the axe above his head. I raised my remaining hand to blast the giant with magical energy, but the Blue Dragon spoke.

"HALT!" the great lizard commanded.

The giants lowered their axes as Dirk rushed over to help me stand.

"Forgive me, Lord Magnus," he said to me. "What is the meaning of this?" he questioned the actions of the three giants that attacked us.

The giants answered Smite in their native tongue.

"I can't understand what they're saying, but if I had to guess, I would say it's not good," Dirk whispered.

"You don't have to know the language," I told him. "Read their thoughts, and you will see what's on their mind."

Smite asked us bluntly, "Did you slay the two giants that guarded the entrance?"

Neither of us answered.

Smite admitted to me, "Your mind is too powerful to read, but your companion's isn't," he added with a crackling smile. The dragon fired a bolt of lightning from his massive jaws, illuminating the cavern in blinding light. My resistance to lightning allowed me to deflect it into the crowd of giants, killing many of them instantly! I quickly fired a bolt of ethereal energy at the dragon, but he magically shielded himself from it.

"THEY ARE IMPOSTERS! OBLITERATE THEM!" Smite commanded of his army. "REDUCE THEIR BONES TO ASH!"

The giant's howled in anticipation of carrying out their master's orders. Their spears and axes magically obtained a burning edge.

"I understood that," Dirk said with a bit of a laugh.

"Perhaps we have overstayed our welcome," I said to him before red leathery wings sprung out from my back, and I flew us above the giants.

Flaming spears were thrown at us, but Dirk pushed them away with telekinetic force. I flew us through the maze of tunnels as we were chased by the army of giants.

Once we made it outside, Fire Giants poured out of the mountain like ants from a mound. I transformed fully into a dragon and turned my fire breath on them. Just as I assumed, it had no effect, but they weren't immune to the power behind a tail whip! I battered our enemies left and right while Dirk fired deadly bolts of ethereal energy.

When it seemed we were about to be surrounded, Dirk climbed onto my back, and I took us up into the air, so it would be easier to evade the giant's flaming spears. I flew us over the terrible giants, so Dirk could continue shooting them with magic missiles.

"Killed another one!" Dirk boasted.

"Great," I congratulated him. "I'll swing back

around so you can kill the rest of them."

"HA! Yeah," Dirk chuckled at my sense of humor.

We then saw Smite emerge from the mountain with a Fire Giant riding on his back! The giant wielded a lance of fire.

I flew high into the early morning sky so that we would be out of range of the giant's on the ground. Dawn would be upon us soon, so I concentrated on creating a blanket of clouds to block out the sun.

"It's not working!" I voiced my frustration.

"What are you trying to do?" Dirk asked.

"I'm trying to gather moisture to create cloud cover."

"We're in a desert," he responded sharply.

I had forgotten where we were and that there wasn't enough moisture to form clouds.

Smite fired a bolt of lightning at us, and I didn't have time to tell Dirk to hold on while I banked away from the attack. After the bolt harmlessly passed by, I asked, "Dirk, are you still with me back there?"

"Yes," he answered sickly. "Warn me before doing that, will you?"

"I'll try," I laughed.

Smite's rider readied his lance as they flew toward us.

"Keep us level," Dirk told me. "I'm going to switch dragons."

"Do you feel confident you can make the jump?"

"I'll make it."

High above the desert sands, I sped toward the great dragon. The Fire Giant sitting upon his back had his burning lance dead set on me, but I stayed the course.

When we were close enough, Dirk ran up the back of my neck and leaped from the tip of my nose toward the dragon rider, wielding an ethereal spear. I quickly transformed back to my human form, so I could get up close and personal with the Fire Giant.

The giant batted Dirk away with his lance, and he slid down the entire length of the enormous Blue Dragon's back before he was able to grab hold of a spike on his tail!

Calling on dragon wings to help me maneuver, I was able to avoid Smite's snapping bite and dodge the giant's lance to get in close. I swung around behind the giant, and while holding onto him with my remaining arm, I bit into his neck to drain what powers I could. He attempted to shake me off, but I spoke to his mind to calm him. "*Shhh, this will be over soon.*"

Smite turned his head and saw that we were on his back. "ANNOYING PESTS!" he said before rolling to throw us off. Dirk was able to maintain his grip, but the giant fell with me still drinking from it.

To the waiting army of Fire Giants far below, I fell, drinking from one of their own. Before hitting the ground, I extended my wings and let the giant fall. Spears once again were thrown at me. One pierced my thigh before I had time enough to deflect it away. The barbed, burning hot spearhead prevented me from removing it easily. I had to push it all the way through my thigh.

In the distance, I saw the colossal Blue Dragon falling from the sky with Dirk not far behind!

Behind me, I heard a growing roar. I turned to see a massive tidal wave sweeping across the desert, consuming the Fire Giants! I flew across the desert to save Dirk from the coming flood!

The dead dragon struck the earth, creating a large crater and expelling sand into the sky. Through the debris, I flew in and caught Dirk's hand, pulling him up into the air as the wall of water passed just beneath us to cleanse the desert! Even the mountains were completely submerged.

"That was a close one," Dirk said to me. "Thank you for the rescue."

Looking west at the morning rays of the sun beginning to peek over the horizon, I reminded him, "You're welcome, but we're not safe yet."

Now, with all the water below us, I concentrated through the searing pain to create storm clouds. I kept us aloft as long as I could above the raging sea waters that now covered the desert as far as the eye could see. Clouds formed to block out the sun but not before my reptilian wings were burned to tatters, and we fell into the sea.

Dirk held onto me, keeping me afloat for the rest of the day. He allowed me to drink from him to help speed my recovery.

After floating for what seemed like hours, I finally asked the big question on my mind. "How were you able to kill Smite?"

"HA! Now that was one scary ride!" he began, remembering the intensity of the conflict. "I was lucky to hang on after the giant struck me. Then I saw you fall, so I felt it was up to me alone to complete the mission. I began by climbing up the dragon's spiny tail, but it kept trying to sling me off. I started to lose my grip, so I focused my thoughts on conjuring swords to dig into the scales at the hip. Smite howled in pain and stopped in midair to grab me. When the beast took hold of me, I felt as if I would be crushed within its grasp. I stabbed its claw, and it loosened its grip just enough for me to slip out. I leaped to its chest where I plunged my ethereal swords in and slid down its belly, slicing the dragon open like gutting an elk."

"Sounds like you fought quite a battle," I commented. "I'm glad you're okay."

"I'm glad we live to fight another day," he added with a smile. "Imagine how quickly we could take back our lands from these monsters if we had an entire legion of vampires under our command."

I did take a moment to envision thousands with our abilities, but the vision took a direction that Dirk did not foresee.

"We should be protective of this power that we've been given," I warned, "or we could one day find ourselves going to war against our own people. We are fighting to preserve the future of mankind for them, not for us. We've had our chance at life. Now, we fight to protect theirs."

For the first time since becoming a vampire, I saw Dirk shed tears. They ran red down his face and were washed away by the sea.

"I miss my family," he said to me. "I miss the life we should have had in the city by the sea. I miss waking up next to my wife and watching my son grow up to be a man. I just wanted a better life for my family, you know? I didn't want my son to have to suffer the same hardships that I did growing up."

"Every father wants a better life for their child."

"Is Eve your only child?" he asked.

"I made her just as I made you. My wife was

unable to have children."

"She was the one that made you immortal?"

"Yes," I answered. "We lived a lifetime together before she revealed to me that she held power over death."

"What happened? Where is she now?" he asked.

"I don't know where she is. We had an argument and she left. She told me that she will be able to see me and will return when the world seemed too much for me to bear."

Dirk looked confused. "Is she invisible? Is she in the sky?"

"Your guess is as good as mine," I answered, shaking my head. "She just disappeared."

"Where did you meet her?"

"We grew up together. Her mother died during childbirth, so my parents raised her."

"Were you ever apart where she could have been made a vampire?"

I took a moment to think back through my long life while we floated in the ocean water. "I can't recall a time, no," I answered honestly.

"What about your parents? What happened to them?"

"My mother died of the fever," I told him, remembering that sad day many years ago. "Vistilia and I were at her bedside when she could no longer fight it. My father died defending the city against Sea Giants."

"That's why you began your quest to eradicate them," Dirk thought aloud.

"I followed in his footsteps, but years later, the giants returned and took the city. Vistilia and I escaped to Athens where we lived out what I thought were the remaining years of our life."

"We both lost a lot to the giants."

"We have," I agreed. "We've lost more than we'll ever know."

"With the power you gained from Ambrosius, are you capable of seeing my life if the Sea Giants didn't ruin it?"

I nodded. "Do you really want to see?"

"I do."

I swam close enough to place my hand on his forehead. I looked into his memories at a time just before his family journeyed south to the port city. I wondered how Dirk's life would play out if they had decided not to leave their home. I allowed him to see the visions as I saw them.

The three families carried out their normal routine. They planted and harvested their crops. They hunted and fished. They cut and stacked firewood. They lived their lives like they had for years . . . until the Storm Giants came. The men fought to protect their families but were no match against the Storm Giant's might. Everyone, including Dirkonus, were killed by the giants that pressed south into more populated regions.

"But the Storm Giants were defeated," Dirk said, wiping his eyes.

I too was curious how the giants made it past our defense, so I turned my vision farther north to the giant's attack on the elves.

Without ever meeting Dirkonus to make him a vampire, I had only Byron to carry into the war against the Storm Giants. The battle played out very similar to how it actually had, until we faced the shamans.

Once again, a shaman grabbed my horns while I

was in dragon form. Byron had his own adversary to deal with, so he was unable to help. The giant got the upper hand and broke my neck! I didn't die, but I was paralyzed from the neck down!

With me out of the fight, poor Byron was outnumbered. While he killed one shaman by spearing him with bolts of ice, another leaped right next to him! He ripped Byron's arms off and took his magical staff!

The shamans maintained the magical protection over their army until they struck Assim from the sky, killing him, and overpowered the Woodland Elves that blocked them from the southern realm.

My dark blood returned the use of my limbs, so I was able to help Byron reattach his arms. While I spent the daylight hours meditating in one of the elves' dwellings, Byron worked to build us an army by raising the dead from the battlefield.

At dusk, we led our army of undead across frozen waters that bridged the northern and southern realms. We tracked the giants for five days before we caught up with them. We ambushed them at their campsite where we finally defeated them, but not before they destroyed two human settlements. One of which was where Dirkonus and his family lived. The huts were left broken and burned from the giants' path of destruction.

"Show no more," I heard Dirk say. "Show no more."

I opened my eyes and pulled my hand from Dirk's forehead. "I'm sorry," I apologized for the visions.

"So it was unavoidable," Dirk said sadly. "My family was doomed either way."

"Do you wish now that you had perished with them?" I asked.

He thought for a moment before answering, "No. I'm thankful for the opportunity and the means to avenge their deaths."

"And I'm thankful I don't have to undertake this quest on my own."

"What are we going to do now that the giants are dead?" he asked.

"We must do what is necessary to save other families from the same fate. We may have vanquished the giants, but there are many more monsters that plague our world. I've heard there are other vampires but none quite like us. Instead of creating others, perhaps we should seek them out and rally them to our cause."

With a nod, my dark son agreed. "We'll need all the help we can get if we are to eliminate the dragons."

The next morning, a speckle of brilliant yellow came into view on the horizon, but it wasn't the sun. I had already blocked out the sun by creating a thick blanket of clouds. As it approached, we were delighted to see it was Assim the Yellow Dragon Lord. He flew over with Byron on his back to rescue us.

"Was that enough water for you?" Byron yelled down to me with a smile stretching from ear to ear.

I gave him a tired smile and a thumbs-up.

Assim reached down and plucked us from the ocean. He then carried us east to the World Council Palace.

CHAPTER XV

UNFORESEEN EVENTS

It didn't take Assim long to fly to the Council Palace. From the looks of it, the main tower had been completed. There were also many more elves and dragons working to build it. The large double doors of the palace tower were standing open for elves to carry in new furniture. Once we landed, Assim took the form of a blond elf and led us inside.

"Remain here," he told us. "I will find out if we're to meet in the Dragon Cavern or in the new council chamber."

Golden wings sprung from his back, and he flew up the center of the tower to the top floor.

The tower was magnificent. It was constructed of marble and had three windows that ran from the floor to the extremely high ceiling where there was a glass roof. A wide walkway spiraled up the tower that led to the many rooms. Looking up at the immensity of the place was breathtaking, to say the least.

"*Are you afraid?*" I heard Dirk's mind ask me telepathically. "*You haven't exactly been doing what these scaleheads sent you to do.*"

"*A little*," I answered honestly, "*but I haven't been gone all that long, so I wouldn't think they've learned yet of my disobedience.*"

"I'm telling you, I can get you a new one," Byron offered, pointing at my missing left arm. "I can have you fixed up as good as new in two shakes of a spriggan's tail."

Both Dirk and I laughed at his offer. "What's a spriggan?" I wondered.

"A spriggan is a kind of fairy that isn't very kind, but they're clever and they're quick, so they can have you fixed in no time."

"No, thank you. It seems to be growing back well enough," I told him, looking over my arm. The elbow had reformed, and I could tell that the radius and ulna were returning beneath the flesh that surrounded them.

After several minutes, Assim returned. "The heads of the council are ready to meet with us."

We began walking up, looking into each of the rooms as we passed by them. We saw elves hanging paintings and bringing flowers into magically lit rooms. They used magic to carve beautifully intricate designs into wood and marble. Those that we met on the walkway welcomed us with a friendly greeting as we continued to the top of the tower.

We reached the double doors of the council chamber where we were to meet with Grimlash, Valik,

Elsbareth, and any new council members that may have been elected.

"What are we going to say about the Giants?" Assim whispered to me.

"We will report that everything is going as planned," I answered calmly. "We will greet the new members, receive our next assignment, and then casually leave."

"All right," he acknowledged.

"I need you two to stay right here," I whispered to Dirk and Byron. "If anything goes wrong, I may need your help."

They both nodded before looking up and down the spiraling walkway for anyone approaching.

Assim opened the doors, and the two of us walked in. There were five identical, bald elves sitting along the backside of the table. The elves quickly thrust their hands out, and I was slammed against the wall where magical chains cuffed my wrist and ankles!

"DIRK!" I called, but when the doors opened, both he and Byron were pushed into the room. They too were chained with unbreakable bonds. A raven-haired Dark Elf with reptilian eyes forced them to stand next to me against the wall where the chains immobilized them. Dirk was chained between me and Byron.

The Dark Elf had confiscated Byron's staff and carefully placed it on the table before the identical elves.

"Ah, the Staff of Storms," one of the bald elves called it.

"You've done well, Valik," another elf said.

"I'm sorry," Dirk apologized, disappointed in himself. "As soon as you walked into the room, these cuffs were slapped on us."

"He flew right up the atrium, taking us by surprise," Byron added, shaking his head.

Byron then yelled at Valik in an ancient dragon language, saying something that I assumed was quite vulgar, for Valik spat in his face! Byron winced as it began liquefying the flesh of his cheek and neck! "Argh! Not the face; I just got it!" he commented painfully.

Valik walked away to stand next to Assim in front of the council table.

I told Dirk and Byron, "I'm the one that should be sorry, not you. I shouldn't have brought you here. If I had taken the time to look into the future at what would transpire, I could have avoided this completely."

"You shouldn't grow so dependent on magic," Dirk warned. "It can only lead to ruin."

"I fear you would've been powerless to change it, even if you did foresee it," Byron broke in, "just as we are powerless to escape these chains."

"I don't believe that," I argued. "The future has many paths."

"Oh, it does," he agreed. "The future has paths beyond count, but if you truly are capable of seeing future events, you are seeing a point where they intersect," he clarified. "There may be different paths to follow, but many of them lead to the same future."

"Excellent work, Assim," I heard the five identical elves say in unison, drawing my attention, and it was then that I realized who they were.

"Grimlash!" I hissed.

The five-headed dragon lord had taken the form of five identical elves to move comfortably within the walls of the World Council Palace.

"When the giants came down from the Cold

Mountains, Woodland Elves did not permit them to cross the ice bridges," one of the five elves explained.

"Accompany Valik to the northern realm and clean up the mess that Magnus made by clearing the road. Kill the elves. Leave none alive to warn their kin," another one of the elves ordered Assim.

"The elven city was all that stood in the way of the Storm Giant's march south into the human territories," the elf sitting at the far end of the table informed them.

"We've already sent Elsbareth to her homeland to mobilize the Giant's cousins, the Trolls, to resume the invasion," the center elf concluded.

"Yes, my lord," both Assim and Valik said with a bow.

"Traiter!" I cursed Assim as he walked by.

He glanced at me with a shameful expression before leaving the room with Valik.

The five elves came around the table to us, and I saw their lower half was that of a snake with the same markings that Grimlash had when I met him in the mountain.

The five elves began searching us for weapons and magical items. The strange, zombie ingredients hanging from Byron's belt were confiscated. Dirk's bronze spear point was taken and tossed on the table with the magical staff.

An elf grabbed Dirk's head and tried to force his mouth open. "Show them to us!" he commanded.

Dirk kept his jaw clenched shut, so the elf punched him. "SHOW THEM!" he yelled, pulling again.

Dirk snapped, biting off a finger and spitting it

in the elf's face! With dark blood on his lips, Dirk laughed, his fangs shining brightly. Another elf moved in and punched him repeatedly. Dirk continued to laugh through the pain.

"Silence your thoughts, so he can't read them," I told Byron and Dirk.

One of the elves punched me in the jaw. "We won't have to read your thoughts."

"Oh, we'll get you to talk," another elf added.

One of them slithered over to a door at the end of the room. When he opened it, Torvin and another Dark Elf from Ashwood stepped in with Eve, bound by the same magical chains that bound us! Her hands were chained behind her, and a short chain connected her ankles. Her hair was a tangled mess, and her arms and face were badly bruised. Her dress was stained with the blood tears that streamed down her face and the abuse she had been dealt.

"EVELYN!" I yelled.

"I WILL KILL ALL OF YOU!" Dirk roared.

We fought against our chains to no avail. They somehow kept us from using our powers! They were metal with a stone set into the cuffs, much like the ones mined from Ashwood.

Torvin was missing his right hand, and he had a disfiguring gash from his left eye to his chin. He shoved Eve to the floor in front of us!

"What strange company you keep, Magnus," the five bald elves that were Grimlash said in unison to me.

"Thank you," he told Torvin and the other elf. "You may leave."

They both bowed before leaving the room, shutting the chamber doors behind them.

Two of the elves picked up Eve and placed her on the table where her chains locked her down. The metal of her cuffs appeared to fuse with the wooden table at the touch of those stones. I tried pressing the stones on my cuffs, but I was not released.

Another elf took a sword down from a plaque that decorated the wall. The sword that he wielded was blue and silver. The blade was definitely obsidian, the volcanic material that the Dark Elves of Ashwood mined. I noticed a strange, crackling sound and a light mist emanating from it.

The other two elves began questioning us. "So, Magnus the Red, now that we have your attention, let us try to clarify this," they began, slithering back and forth in front of us. "You somehow convinced Ambrosius the Yellow to nominate you for a seat on our council. After which, you killed him. Once you received your orders to aid the three races of Giants, you instead eradicated the Sea Giants using an army of the dead that this necromancer summoned. You killed the Storm Giant shamans that provided mystical protection to their race, and then used the dead giants to fight against their own forces. While Assim fought on the frontlines against Woodland Elves, you were eliminating his army from the rear. You then proceeded to the mountains where the Fire Giants dwell, and you used the Staff of Storms to flood the entire country! By the time Assim was able to catch up with you, you had nearly single-handedly driven the race of Giants to extinction. Does that sound like an accurate account to you?" He stared directly into my eyes.

"Did you hear this from Assim?" I asked.

"Yes."

"Then Assim is a liar," I told him.

"Did you, Magnus, or did you not kill the giants that you were specifically ordered to assist?" Grimlash asked angrily.

"You're planning to kill them all anyway," I argued.

"But there's an order that must be followed, so the war is not brought to our doorstep," the bald elf leader explained.

"What? Can you not handle the world at your doorstep?" Dirk asked through an arrogant smile, taunting him.

He was punched again but chuckled while blood oozed from his mouth, dripping to the marble floor.

"Dirk, we're in no position to be taunting these snakes," Byron commented, his jawbone visible where the flesh of his face had melted from Valik's corrosive saliva.

"We are Grimlash," the five elves announced together, seemingly offended being called snakes. "We are the last of the legendary Hydra race."

Bitterly, I asked, "What makes you think you are capable of managing an entire world of races when you can't even manage your own?"

"We will restore my race to its former glory by resurrecting them from the grave, and you will help us," Grimlash asserted. "Which brings us to this little girl," the five elves said, turning to Eve.

"Let her go!" Dirk commanded.

"We're afraid not, my young vampire," one of the elves said with a smile. "There are many vampires in the world, but we want to find the source. We want to learn the secret to true immortality." He grabbed Dirk by the throat. "Who made you, vampire? Who turned this little girl?"

"Suck you!" Dirk cursed, spitting blood in Grimlash's face.

The sword-wielding elf raised his blade over Eve.

"I did it!" I answered before he harmed my little girl.

All five of the half-elf serpents turned their attention to me. "You lie!" one of them barked, slithering over to me. Looking into my eyes, he could see that I was telling the truth. "How? How was it done?"

"Through the blood," I answered.

"But this blood must have the power to preserve life," he argued. "How did you attain this power?"

Thoughts of what could happen next flooded my mind. I imagined Grimlash using Byron's zombie ingredients to raise his fallen brethren from the dead and using my blood to heal their flesh. The Hydras could rule the entire Earth forever!

I was slow to answer his question, so the sword was raised again to kill Eve!

"It was a woman!" I answered quickly before it was too late.

"What woman?" Grimlash asked, intimidating me with his proximity. "Where is she now?"

"I don't know where she is," I answered truthfully.

His expression turned angrily disappointed. Suddenly, the elf swung his sword and completely severed Eve's right leg! A heart wrenching scream spilled from her lungs as her leg turned cold and brittle!

"You monster, release her! I told you the truth!" I yelled, with tears filling my eyes.

He punched me again in the face! "The elves of Ashwood didn't take kindly to you leaving this vampire in their city to feed upon them. If you're not going to tell us what we wish to know, then we will make an example of you to the other dragons when they arrive tomorrow." He turned to look at Eve crying on the table, "But for this little one, you will watch her die."

"I'LL KILL YOU!" I roared.

"She is innocent!" Dirk cried.

"Let the girl go," Byron pleaded. "You have us to study."

"Oh, you will be studied," one of the elves said with a menacing smile, "from the inside out."

"Our army will stretch across the land," another elf informed us. "The witch that you claim bestowed this power upon you will be found. All secrets will be uncovered soon enough."

Another swing of the frost blade took Eve's other leg!

"AHHH!" she screamed.

I pulled with all of my might against my chains! I even tried turning into a dragon to break them, but I could not. I was unable to save Evelyn from torture.

"DADDY, HELP ME!" she cried.

The elf chopped away her right arm!

"DIRK! BROTHER!" she yelled out for his help as the cold slowly consumed her.

"STOP!" Dirk begged. "PLEASE STOP!"

"Vistilia!" I prayed. "Come back! Save our little girl!" I begged.

One of the elves slithered back to me. "Where is

this Vistilia? Do you think she'll come to save this bloodthirsty monster?" he asked.

Ignoring him, I continued to ask for Vistilia's help. "Please, Vistilia, my love, I beg you to help us. Please, save us from this torturous evil."

The five bald elves looked around the room, half expecting something to happen. One even slithered to the large window to look for anyone that may come to save us, but there was no one.

"It would appear that Vistilia, this god you pray to, has abandoned you to torment," one of the elves scoffed. He reached out to catch the magical sword that was tossed to him.

"No," I said to him. "Don't do this."

He raised the blade!

"NO!" I yelled.

He swung, decapitating my beloved Sunshine! The chains were released, and with the thrust of a hand, he magically hurled her through the glass into the midday sun where she burned to ash and was scattered by the breeze!

I screamed out in agony and collapsed. I hung from my chains, a broken man. Crimson tears streamed down my face.

I heard one of the terrible elves say, "No other council member will rebel after an example is made of you."

The elf wielding the obsidian sword leaned in close before speaking to me. "The pain you feel now is nothing compared to what the three of you will feel tomorrow."

He pressed the tip of the sword against my cheek. I felt a cold so intense that it burned, but I had no emotion left to show him. He cut a line down my face before he and the other four identical elves slithered from the room.

Dirk and I hung quietly from our chains. We had no fight left within us.

"That girl did not deserve death," Byron said sadly.

CHAPTER XVI

MAGNUS VS GRIMLASH

Late that evening, the council chamber doors opened, but it wasn't Grimlash coming to interrogate us. It was Assim! He rushed in and touched each of the stones on our chains. One by one, the cuffs released until the three of us were free.

I fell to the floor, but Dirk grabbed Assim by the throat and slammed him against the wall!

"You betrayed us!" Dirk spat. While choking him with his right hand, he called upon two ethereal blades that extended from his left fist. "He killed my sister!"

"I didn't know," Assim strained to say.

"You lied about your involvement to save your own ass!" Byron accused.

"They . . . would've found out . . . the truth soon . . . anyway," Assim muttered. "We don't . . . have much time."

"Dirk, release him," I commanded before rolling over on my back.

He did as I asked, releasing his grip on Assim's throat but kept his ethereal blades in case he needed them.

Byron helped me to my feet while Assim caught his breath.

"Why are you helping us escape?" I asked him.

Breathing deeply, Assim answered, "Because it won't take long for Grimlash to learn that I aided you in your fight against the Giants. Yes, I lied to save my ass, but I would not be able to help you now if I too were chained. But we cannot linger; Valik will soon be here. We must kill Grimlash."

"Where is he?" I asked fiercely.

"He's in the Dragon Cavern, but you cannot fight him in your condition."

"Then let me drink your blood," I asked of him without thinking of keeping my secret.

With a look of confusion, he asked, "What?"

"Blood gives me strength," I explained. "It heals me. I only need a little," I assured him.

He agreed with a nod, so I took hold of his arm. My fangs extended, and I pierced the flesh. It seemed there was no end to his veins. As I took long draughts of his blood, I closed my eyes to focus not on Assim's thoughts but on the future. I saw what I must do and the consequences that follow.

When I had drank enough to satisfy my hunger, I saw that my arm had grown back, and my hand was quickly returning. "Thank you," I told him. "Thank you for coming back for us."

"You are welcome," he said with a bow. "Thank you for helping me to defeat the giants. Thank you all."

Dirk reclaimed his bronze spearhead from the table and tied it to his belt. Eager to exact revenge for the murder of his beloved sister, he said, "Now, to kill that accursed Grimlash!"

"No, my son," I stopped him. "You will be the last. I need you to finish what we have begun. The future belongs to the humans."

"The humans?" Assim repeated, not believing his ears.

"Yes, they are the rightful heirs of the Earth," I explained. Turning back to Dirk and Byron, I told them, "Create an army in secrecy, and do what is necessary to ensure the fate of humanity."

"But Magnus, you cannot do this alone," Dirk began to argue. "Let us fight with you, and we can defeat Grimlash together."

"I'm sorry," I apologized, "but this is how it's supposed to be. I must face Grimlash alone, and you are to stay as far away from here as possible. If you are discovered, the dragons will learn the secret of immortality, and they will be invincible. We cannot let that happen."

"Very well," he nodded sadly.

I shook Byron's hand and thanked him for his help. "Farewell, my friend."

"Farewell."

I then hugged my son goodbye.

"I will not fail you," Dirk promised.

"Do not fail our people," I corrected him, placing a hand on his shoulder.

Turning to Assim, I told him, "Get them to

safety."

"Very well," he acknowledged. "Good luck."

"Good luck to you," I responded.

Assim walked over to the broken window and motioned for Byron and Dirk to hurry. Byron quickly gathered his ingredient pouches from the table before they leaped out of the window. Assim transformed into a Yellow Dragon and flew off into the moonless night sky carrying Dirk and Byron on his back.

I took a deep breath and jumped out the window. My Red Dragon wings carried me across the valley and up the mountainside to the Dragon Cavern entrance. I flew through the cave to the large room where the dragon lords held meetings for millennia. The room was magically lit by several glowing orbs. Grimlash was at the large, stone table in his dragon form with his back to the entrance. I summoned a long, ethereal spear and flew toward him. The mystical weapon was dead set on my enemy, but he vanished at the very moment before impaling him!

Standing on the table, I looked around the room but saw nothing. I heard nothing. I changed my spear to a sword and shield. Suddenly, a large shape appeared next to me, and I was struck with enough force to shatter my bones if I had not held a phantom shield to take the blow! I was knocked clear across the chamber.

"How did you escape your bonds?" I heard two of his heads ask in unison. "No matter," the others added.

Before I could get to my feet, I was surprised by him again when he snatched me up.

"It seems we won't be making an example of you after all," he laughed.

I quickly brought my shield up to block one of his fearsome snake heads from striking me! Through its ghostly transparency, I saw another head smash into the shield. His fangs were longer than my sword! While one head pushed against my shield, the others sought to flank my defense. I couldn't fight him like this. I needed to change. After fighting off his attacks for a moment longer, I began my transformation into a Red Dragon. He lost his grip on me and was knocked away by my tail. I breathed fire at him, but he teleported to safety.

"You have great power, human," Grimlash's voice echoed from somewhere in the mountain. "Your god may have once favored you, but your life now resides within our grip."

I opened my mouth to speak, but I was suddenly bound by Grimlash! I lost my balance and fell. His body was coiled tightly around me, constricting my muscles. When I exhaled, he squeezed all the more tighter. I then felt many fangs striking my neck, and a burning sensation swept through my body. I involuntarily reverted back to human form and slipped from Grimlash's crushing grip. I stumbled away from him, but he didn't give chase. He simply watched as his venom ran its lethal course.

This venom wasn't like the venom from the adders of Greece. It didn't bring paralysis, no. It brought putridity! My skin began to peel as layers of tissue liquefied and fell away. The necrosis spread like wildfire, leaving blackened, dead flesh in its wake!

I watched in horror as my body shriveled to that of a corpse. When my legs could no longer support me, I crumpled to the floor. My muscles stopped convulsing, and my breathing waned. I felt my heart shudder for a moment, but it continued to keep my mind alert while it fought to endure the dreadful toxin.

The towering serpent slithered near, over-shadowing me. "You know, Magnus, you're just the right size for a midnight snack," his center head hissed, bringing a disturbing laugh from the others.

I inhaled deeply as the strength of my lungs returned, and it was then that I saw Dirk approaching from the air behind him, wielding a large, ethereal axe! He buried the axe into Grimlash's center head, splitting it in two! With an ear piercing shriek, Grimlash's body distorted, and the four living heads separated from the dead one.

Dirk rushed to my aid. "Magnus, can you hear me?"

A raspy, unintelligible voice escaped me.

He bit his wrist and placed it to my lips. My body absorbed his blood like water into a sponge, and the poison in my veins was dispelled.

Byron ran into the chamber and fired a bolt of lightning from his staff. The lightning struck one of the large snakes and arced to another. The remaining two snakes lunged at him. Assim entered the room just in time to snatch up the closest snake in his massive jaws! The second snake sank its fangs into Byron, injecting Grimlash's terrible venom.

The two snakes that were hit by lightning were stunned but quickly shook it off. They took the form of bald elves like before but kept their dragon wings, so they could fly if needed.

Byron looked down at his torso where he had white venom oozing from two large puncture wounds! "HAHAHAHAA! Magic circulates this body, not blood," he told the perplexed Grimlash before blasting him with lightning. While the bolt of electricity arced between the head of the staff and Byron's attacker, he plunged the butt end of the staff into the rocky floor of the cavern. The ground opened to devour the large serpent!

After drinking a bit more blood from Dirk, I regained the use of my legs and was able to stand. "I'm glad you didn't listen to me," I told him, "but you really do need to get far away from this place before the others arrive."

Before he could argue with me, one of the bald elves teleported behind him and attempted to bite him. His mouth opened wide, and long fangs sprang forward. I pushed him with telekinetic force against the cave wall. Dirk summoned an ethereal axe and split the slithering elf in half at the waist! Pinned against the wall, Grimlash hissed. Dirk pulled his axe free and swung it again to chop off his head!

"There's still one left," I told everyone.

Assim took the form of an elf, and the four of us stood back to back in the center of the room.

"Show yourself!" I yelled.

Not Grimlash but Valik came into the cavern! Our eyes widened at the sight of the menacing Black Dragon, for we were hoping to be gone before he returned. Seeing that we were bunched together, he didn't waste any time with words. He belched up a mouthful of his highly corrosive saliva and spat it at us! Both Dirk and I created a force field of telekinetic energy to block the spray of acid from our companions.

"Dirk," I yelled, "you need to get out of here!"

"I'm not leaving without you," he argued.

"We're going to need your help if we are to save the world."

Valik charged toward us, causing us to divide. He whipped his tail, knocking Byron across the room.

With no time to argue with Dirk, I turned to Assim. "Get them out of here, Assim!"

"What about you?"

"I must stay behind to kill Grimlash," I told him.

Across the room, I saw Valik biting and swatting at Dirk while Byron was using the Staff of Storms to form a tornado.

Assim changed into a Yellow Dragon and leaped on Valik! Dirk stumbled to get out of the way as the two massive serpents clawed at each other. Fire roared and acid spewed from their mouths, but neither caused much harm to the other. The cavern, though, looked like a death trap!

Byron directed his tornado into the council table to break it into large chunks of rock. He then sent it into battle against the Black Dragon Lord. The tornado slammed Valik with the rock and debris that it had picked up!

I ran to pull Dirk to safety, but Grimlash appeared before me in his half-elf form! He lunged at me with the frost sword, but I was quick enough to sidestep the attack. I grabbed hold of his wrists to wrestle the sword away from him. Dirk moved in to kill him while I held his attention, but I was suddenly blinded by a bright flash of light.

I heard Dirk yell, "MAGNUS!" but then his voice sounded far away. My eyes adjusted to find that Grimlash had teleported us to the top of the Council Palace tower!

I summoned a two handed sword to combat him. He swung at me, but when I blocked his sword with mine, I didn't cut through it as I expected. The obsidian sword had been magically imbued to hold its strength.

Flapping his wings, he lifted himself up and tail whipped me across the chest! I fell backwards onto the large, glass skylight of the palace. He swung the frost blade at me, but I was able to block the attack with my ethereal sword. Glancing below me, I could see elves within the tower pointing up at us.

"I don't know how you survived my bite, but you will never have control of the Earth, human," Grimlash spat. "It is mine alone to rule! Your kind is nothing more than food for the Dragons."

"I survived because I AM IMMORTAL!"

With all my strength, I pushed him away from me. I ran toward him, rolled beneath his attack, and locked my arms around his from behind him.

"And I have a bite of my own!" I revealed, sinking my fangs into his neck and searching his mind for untold power.

He tried to shake me off but could not. He used his wings to carry us high above the tower, but I did not let go. He began growing in size as he took his true form. I was forced to retract my fangs when the flesh beneath them became scales, but I held on. Since his other four heads had been destroyed, he now had only one left.

He made a quick spiral in the air, causing me to lose my grip on his now smooth skin. While tumbling back to the tower rooftop, I called out my dragon wings to keep me aloft, but they were still mangled and deformed from his deadly toxin.

Above, Grimlash folded his wings back and

dove toward me. His gaping jaws were set to swallow me whole! Spotting the obsidian sword that seemed tiny now within his grasp, I telekinetically pulled it from his hand to mine. He quickly spread his wings to halt his descent. I then used the power that I stole through the drinking of his blood to teleport above him!

"DIE, SHITHEAD!" I cursed, plunging the sword deep into his skull!

Grimlash released an ear piercing shrill of anguish as the obsidian sword's power took hold, freezing his entire body. Before I could teleport to safety, we crashed through the skylight of the tower! We plummeted to the bottom where Grimlash, head dragon of the World Council, shattered across the floor. The impact knocked me unconscious.

CHAPTER XVII

IMPRISONED WITHIN THE EARTH

The darkness of unconsciousness faded when I was lifted from the palace floor. There were many elves surrounding me. Grimlash's broken body was scattered about. I attempted to teleport away, but the power was unresponsive. I then realized my hands and feet were bound by the same magic infused chains that held me before.

I was held up by two Woodland Elves. A white-haired female elf approached and grabbed me by the throat. She too appeared to be a Woodland Elf but her white, reptilian eyes told me that she was Elsbareth the White Dragon Lord.

"Magnus the Red," she addressed me. "You nearly destroyed the World Council in one night. You killed Valik in the ancient Dragon Cavern. You then came here and killed Grimlash. I assume you killed

Assim, for he is missing. Would you have killed me as well, if I were present?"

"Yes," I uttered beneath her grip.

Before releasing me, she punched me three times in the face. I spat blood at her feet.

"How could you turn on your own kind?" she asked, not knowing the truth as Grimlash did.

"Grimlash murdered my little girl," I explained.

"So you began eliminating the council members?"

"You all are tyrants!" I yelled.

She grabbed me by the hair and pulled me away from the elves that held me. She then slammed my face into the floor and stomped me!

"Why do you take human form?" she asked as I lay beneath her bare foot. "They are an ignorant race of filthy savages."

"How are you any better?" I uttered. "You, who pose as an elf, yet secretly plan to choke their race from existence."

"SHUT UP!" she kicked me again.

"Is there truth to what Lord Magnus says?" one of the elves asked her.

"HAHAHAA!" I laughed at her. "The seed has been planted. HAHAHAA!"

"Lady Elsbareth?" the elf demanded an answer.

"Heed not the lies of this traitor!" she spat.

Furious, she grabbed me by the throat and lifted me off the floor.

"Go ahead, kill me," I told her, gurgling on my own blood. "I don't care anymore."

"No. Oh no," she smiled. "You won't be getting out that easily. You will suffer for your crimes."

"Do what you will with me," I told her.

Smiling, she repeated, "What I will."

She dragged me outside where she took dragon form and carried me off into the night. She flew a great distance before landing on the edge of a volcano.

"Since ancient times, our fallen brethren have often been returned to the earth from this very spot," she told me. "The great Shadowrath himself was even cast in here at the end of the Draconian Wars. You should feel honored to be imprisoned within the Abyss of the Dead. I can only imagine what awaits you beyond the Infernal Waves. Will the dead greet you upon the Black Shore, or will you drown in the Lake of Chaos?"

I wished for the sun to break through the night sky and spare me the torment that awaited me, but the sun did not come. I silently spoke to Vistilia to save me, but my pleas went unanswered. I was alone.

Elsbareth spoke in an ancient, dark tongue that thundered throughout the mountainous region. The sky seemed to split open with a terrible storm and lightning lit the sky with a bolt that plunged into the abyss before me.

She transformed back into an elf and kissed my lips! This wasn't just any farewell kiss, mind you. This kiss brought the icy cold breath that the White Dragons were feared for having. Her lips brought a burning cold like Grimlash's sword except it consumed my body as quickly as his venom. I felt my dark blood slow to a crawl within my veins, and my thoughts dulled as Elsbareth's kiss of death chilled me to the bone.

She removed the chains that bound my hands and feet, but the kiss she gave prevented me from focusing the power necessary to escape. My knees buckled under the weight of my own body, and I collapsed, powerless at the dragon lord's feet.

"Forgive me for not being one for long goodbyes," she apologized coldly before tossing me into the volcano.

Into the Abyss of the Dead, I fell, and darkness soon surrounded me. It was a darkness even my vampire eyes could not penetrate. I felt the chill of Elsbareth's kiss fade, but I still could not teleport to safety! I could not fly! It felt as if I was being pulled into the void.

Grimlash and Valik were dead. I could only hope that Assim was able to get Dirk and Byron to safety. They would have to carry on without me.

"Oh, my dear Evelyn," I said aloud. "I'm sorry I couldn't save you. Your death was my fault," I cried. "I became so wrapped up in changing the world that I lost sight of what was most precious to me, family. I even saw my imprisonment if I followed through with my plan, but it didn't deter me from what I believed I must do. I didn't think about how my actions would affect you. I'm sorry, Sunshine. I would undo it all to give you the life you deserve."

A speck of light came into view far below me! As I fell and approached the light, I saw that not a city of elves awaited me but a lake of fire! A terrible roar and a great heat grew within the cavernous expanse. The walls of the volcano were now illuminated like embers in a fire. I tried to steer my descent toward the cavern wall, but I could not. I was being drawn into this torment, and its pull was too great to resist. My only hope now was that the boiling lake would bring death quickly.

On instinct, I inhaled deeply and closed my eyes

before plunging into what Elsbareth called the Lake of Chaos, but death did not come. My body was resisting the intense heat! I either absorbed this resistance to fire from the dragon rider that I drank from in the desert or from Ambrosius, but beneath these turbulent waters, I could feel it slowly penetrating my defense.

If I couldn't use my power to escape or control my direction, I thought, perhaps I could at least shield myself. Focusing what strength I still had, I felt the energy from my body's core expand to push the incinerating magma away from my skin. It was working! I maintained my focus to continue feeding energy into the magical barrier while I was pulled deeper within the Earth!

After hours, maybe days, of maintaining the energy field around me, I felt my concentration waning; I needed to feed! With my hands against the barrier, I struggled to hold it together. I knew I was being drawn deep into the planet, but around me, I saw only the coursing, undrinkable blood of the Earth.

I felt my nose begin to bleed beneath the strain, and tears of blood broke from my eyes as I fought to keep the lava from destroying me.

"I can't hold this shield forever, and I can't escape to drink the blood I need to sustain myself," I said to myself. "I destroyed the Giants and reclaimed Crete as I set out to do. I just wish I could rebuild Atronos, and live there peacefully with Vistilia and our little girl, Evelyn. I love you both."

No longer able to maintain the spell that protected me, the Lake of Chaos penetrated my magical sphere. The burning waters once again made contact with my bare skin and continued to erode my resistance.

With the searing pain rising, I expected my immortal life to soon be stripped away, but my face broke through the surface of the lake! I opened my eyes to see that I was in an immense cavern beyond measure. The thick, rolling waves washed me ashore where I clawed at black sand to drag my scorched body away from the terrible waters. I finally collapsed, unable to go any further. I was mentally and physically exhausted.

"Well, there you are," a familiar voice woke me.

I lifted my head to see clean feet mere inches from my face. The person sat down on the black sand to hold me in their arms, and my eyes finally focused on her beautiful face. Vistilia had come back to me!

"You've come a long way," she said, carefully rubbing my charred forehead.

"A long way?" I repeated. "I've lost every-thing."

"You have steered the world toward an exciting new future," she praised.

"But I pushed you away, and I caused Evelyn's death!"

"You chose a path that no other could choose," she stated. "It has been difficult, and you've lost much, but don't despair; no one is lost forever."

"What do you mean?" I asked, looking up at her. "Can you bring Evelyn back from the dead the same as you did me?"

Smiling warmly, she said, "Your heart is in the right place. You asked to give her life instead of saving you from this torment."

"Evelyn should not have suffered for my mistakes," I cried.

Vistilia was suddenly saddened by this. "Don't blame yourself for Evelyn's death; it was not your fault. Paths often hold unforeseeable events."

"But you have the power to set everything right," I uttered.

"One thing I've learned since studying the human race from this perspective is that we are too quick to ask for help from a higher power when the purpose of life is to live and learn. The universes are cruel and unjust. If there are gods, they care not for our petty troubles and do not barter wishes for sacrifices. Instead of looking up to beings that may or may not exist, we should look within ourselves for how we can contribute to shaping our universe into a better place."

I was too weak to argue with her anymore, so she continued. "I'm proud of you for doing just that," she said to me. "Evelyn's people loved their god and their king more than they loved their own children. Kings should take care of their people. Gods should take care of their space. You gave that little girl more time to live. That was more than anyone else could do for her. You've done the same for the entire world by removing Grimlash from power."

I said nothing. I lay limp in her arms, utterly exhausted.

"You need to start eating better. You're just skin and bones," she commented, bringing a weak laugh from me.

She held me close, and my fangs broke through the supple flesh of her neck. The precious elixir of life flowed into me, instantly restoring my vitality and healing my charred body. I probed for her thoughts, but like before, I heard nothing, I saw nothing. Her mind was closed to me. I drank to my heart's content before retracting my fangs and standing on my own.

"Thank you," I told her, standing naked on the Black Shore. "Thank you for saving me. I would have starved without your blood. You have provided that which I needed."

"You may have been imprisoned within the Earth for 151 years, but you are not alone."

"Excuse me. What was that?" I asked, using my little finger to clean the sand from my ear. "I thought I heard you say that I've been down here for 151 years."

"Yes," she answered. "You died of thirst after pulling yourself ashore."

Rubbing my head, I walked away from her. "Great! That's just great! Well, I'm glad you came to wake me up."

"Oh, you're welcome, sweetheart. I'll stay for a short while before you go back to sleep," she said, ignoring my sarcasm.

"But I don't need to go back to sleep; I have work to do."

She then pointed across the dark beach to the blackness that lay beyond. "Then you may want to take a look around."

I stepped away from her, walking in the direction that she pointed, but my eyes saw nothing in the darkness. "What is in there?" I asked. "Is it a way out?"

I turned away from the darkness to behold a striking scene like no other. My beautiful Vistilia, with her olive skin and raven hair, stood on a black, sandy beach, wearing a white dress with an ocean of magma behind her.

"You are a goddess," I whispered. "I'm sorry for being angry with you all those years ago," I apologized sincerely.

"And I'm sorry the universe is as it is," she said, walking over to me, her hair and dress blowing from the swirling heat. "You cannot return to the surface until the spell is broken from above," she explained.

"So we have some time," I said, kissing the love of my life. "I can't think of a better punishment than being banished to a dark beach with you."

After an undetermined amount of time with Vistilia, I decided it was time to venture into the darkness. At the far end of the Black Shore, there was a wall of stone where cool air blew into the cavern through a carved archway with runic symbols etched around its border.

"What manner of being could survive at such depths?" I asked as I ran my fingers over the symbols.

Taking Vistilia's hand in mine, we slowly ventured into the passageway. My vampire eyes were finally able to cut through the darkness, but she preferred some light.

"All this darkness is depressing," she commented before materializing burning torches along the walls with a snap of her fingers.

As we explored, I began telling her what had happened since she left, but it became clear to me that she already knew what happened. She had indeed been watching over me during her absence.

We seemed to be in an abandoned mine, though no tools were found. We wandered the corridors and empty rooms for days, finding no way out.

"Who dug these tunnels?" I pondered while Vistilia and I sat on the beach. "How did they get down here, and where did they go?"

"Perhaps you missed something," she said, looking out over the rolling waves of molten rock.

"I didn't miss anything. We searched everywhere." I then remembered who I was talking to and realized that she knew that I missed something. "So what did I miss?"

She drew a circle in the black sand with her finger and struck it with a bolt of lightning from her hand. She then lifted a circular piece of glass from the sand and handed it to me.

"What's this for?" I asked, noticing lines and shapes scratched into the glass.

"It's a map of everywhere we explored."

"Amazing."

After looking over it for a few minutes, I noticed that there was a large middle area that we hadn't explored.

"I wonder why we didn't see this area. Let's go take a look."

Carrying the glass map, Vistilia and I headed back into the mine. We circled the area but found no entrance. We did, however, find what once used to be a doorway, but it had been sealed off.

"Ah ha! I did miss something."

"You would have eventually noticed this door," Vistilia commented.

"Yeah, eventually," I repeated with a smile.

I handed her the map and created an ethereal sword to cut around several of the blocks that sealed the large door. I then used telekinesis to carefully pull the blocks out.

"You shouldn't need this anymore," Vistilia said about the map. She bumped it with her fist, and the glass turned back into sand.

We entered the room, which was already lit by torches, but we seemed to be behind a massive statue. We walked around to the front to see that it was a statue of a large bird holding down a terrible dragon!

"This must be Arethil and Shadowrath," I said, looking over the statue.

Sitting in front on an ornate pedestal was a large chest carved out of the same stone that the elves of Ashwood mined. The chest was black as pitch, and upon lifting the lid, I saw that it was full of bones! Positioned neatly on top was a bird's skull that was about a foot long.

Disappointedly, I said, "I imagined her to be bigger."

"Statues are rarely carved to actual size," Vistilia said as she strolled around the large room, looking at the many statues that lined the other walls.

"I was talking about the remains," I clarified, but she was preoccupied with the statues.

The room held many long, wooden tables with chairs. Statues of stout, bearded men lined the left and right walls. They looked kingly and proud, wearing circlets upon their thick brows and holding great hammers. At the far end of the room was a stone staircase leading up to another level!

"Vistilia, honey, we're heading up," I said excitedly.

"*You need to get Arethil's remains to the surface.*"

"What did you say?" I asked Vistilia, who was already at the stairs.

She giggled and said, "I didn't say anything. That was in your head."

"So I have been hearing Ambrosius' voice!" I exclaimed. "How is this possible?"

"Do you remember the mixture he drank before you killed him?"

"Vaguely," I answered.

"It allowed all of his thoughts and memories to be taken by you but held together so that he can still think and speak to you."

I stood there absolutely speechless.

With a smile, she added, "You didn't think he would ask a stranger to carry out a near impossible task without overseeing their progress from time to time, did you?"

Thinking a moment about what I needed to do, I finally said, "Well, I suppose we should take this with us because it is a very long way to the surface. I sure don't want to try carrying it out the way I came in."

"You won't be able to leave," Vistilia reminded me. "The spell cast over you will block your escape well before reaching the surface."

"Well, I'll just have to figure out something when I reach my limit."

As soon as I picked up the obsidian chest filled with Arethil's remains, I saw the pedestal it was on begin to raise, and we heard a heavy bell ring from somewhere in the tunnels above us.

"Ah, Hades!" I cursed. I then set the chest back on its pedestal and waited for whoever the bell alerted.

Hearing soldiers approaching, Vistilia and I took

a seat at a table facing the stairs. Two dozen stocky soldiers rushed down the stairs wearing thick armor and wielding large hammers. They all had thick beards that ranged in color from red to blond. Some were braided while others hung loose.

I held my hands out to show that I was unarmed while the soldiers quickly surrounded us. I found it amusing that, even sitting down, I was taller than they were, but I held back my laughter.

"Good evening," I greeted them with a smile. "Or is it good morning?"

"Living at these depths, I doubt they even know," Vistilia whispered to me.

"Right," I agreed.

The one directly in front of me yelled in a thick, angry tongue, but I didn't have to know the language to understand he was asking how I got into this room. I pointed behind me, so my interrogator sent one of his soldiers to take a look behind the statue.

The soldier reported what he found, and we were ordered to our feet. Vistilia and I were then escorted up the stairs, down a long hallway, and up another set of stairs where we were led to a large room to meet the king of their people. Two of the soldiers stood by their king and watched over us while another two stood behind us.

The king held his hands out, palms up, so I placed my hands on his. He gave a bow and spoke to me in a language I understood. "Have a seat," he said, motioning to a table loaded with all sorts of food.

He looked like the others except he was much older and wore nice clothing instead of armor. His hair was white, and his beard was neatly trimmed.

The room we were in was elaborately furnished with animal furs on the floor, well-crafted weapons and armor hanging on the walls, and statues standing in the corners. A roaring fire warmed the cold, stone room.

"Help yourself," he said as he filled his plate with a turkey leg, cranberries, and a steaming hot potato.

A woman of their hardy race walked into the room bringing four large mugs of mead. She leaned in close to the king for a kiss before sitting beside him at the table.

I didn't take any food, but Vistilia piled her plate full.

"I am the Dwarf King Wendale, and this is my wife, Rosalie."

"How do you do?" the lady greeted.

"So how do two humans make it to the Black Shore?" the king asked as he casually cut open his potato.

The woman sitting next to him looked up from her plate in shock. "And without a mark to show for it," she added.

"They're wizards, dear," King Wendale told his wife.

"WIZARDS!" she repeated with a gasp. "My goodness!"

The four guards swallowed nervously and gripped their hammers tighter.

"I am Lord Magnus of the World Council, and this is my wife, Vistilia," I announced, remembering to change my eyes to look reptilian.

"A dragon!" Wendale spat while taking a big bite from his turkey leg.

The guards immediately dropped to the floor and

covered their heads with their hands.

"This tale is getting better by the minute," the king added enthusiastically, glancing down at his cowardly guards. "What brings you and your wife down here, Lord Magnus?"

"A powerful wizard named Ambrosius has sent me to bring Arethil's remains to the surface."

"The Ambrosius?" he asked, surprised. "The elf from legend?"

"The very same," I answered with a smile.

"HAHAA!" the dwarf king laughed. "So the legends are true. I suppose one can't be a powerful wizard without having power, now can they?"

I laughed at his analogy. "I suppose not."

He then waved his guards away now that he felt comfortable with us. They picked themselves up from the floor and waited by the door in case they were needed.

Vistilia cleaned her plate and began filling it up again with venison, potatoes, carrots, green beans, and a couple bread rolls.

"Why, it's nice to see a girl with a healthy appetite," Rosalie commented, reaching over to pat Vistilia's hand. "This kind of food will put some meat on your bones, so you can keep your man warm at night."

"Food is the one thing we dwarves are not short on!" Wendale boasted.

"Tell me about it," Rosalie whispered across the table.

Vistilia burst into laughter, spraying potatoes from her mouth and bringing a laugh from all of us! She leaned her head against my shoulder while we all chuckled.

"Got away with you did it, sweetie?" Rosalie asked, still laughing.

"Yes. It caught me off guard," my wife answered with a nod, wiping the tears from her eyes.

"Lord Magnus, why aren't you eating?" Rosalie asked, looking over at my empty plate. "Don't think this is all we have. We have more than enough food to feed a hungry dragon."

"This sort of cuisine doesn't satisfy my husband's appetite," Vistilia answered her.

Wendale coughed as he voiced his concern. "I hope dwarves neither."

I only laughed because I couldn't tell them the truth. I couldn't tell them that I was really a bloodthirsty vampire and that I planned to drink from them while they slept.

"You and your people will be just fine," Vistilia assured them with a smile that only I recognized as devious.

"Well then, as long as we'll be fine, we should return to business," Wendale announced, wiping his mouth with a napkin. "So what can my people do to assist you, Lord Magnus?"

"Do you have a map?"

Wendale stood up and motioned for me to follow him to a small table across the room where he had a stack of parchment. "Under or above ground?" he asked.

"Above."

He lifted a few to look at what was drawn on them before pulling one out to place on top of the stack.

I studied over the map for a moment to pinpoint

a specific place. "I need a group of your finest soldiers to carry Arethil's remains to a human settlement here," I said, pointing to the general location. "Have them follow a mountain trail to an ancient castle. In the throne room of this castle, there is a tunnel that leads deep below ground. Call down into the tunnel for King Byron. It is imperative that he gets it."

"I will gather my men and relay the orders."

"Why are you helping me?" I asked, suddenly curious.

Walking back to the dinner table, he said, "When my ancestors heard that Arethil's remains were locked within an obsidian chest and cast into the earth, they tunneled down in search of her. They knew that one day she would be called to the surface, and until that day, we would keep her safe. But there is a small matter that needs taken care of first."

"Name it," I said as we took our seats.

"I'm almost embarrassed to say this, but many of the upper levels of our tunnel system have recently become infested with goblins. We'll need to break through their nesting area, so we can get outside."

They must be some of the goblins that Elsbareth has been using to invade and weaken other races, I thought to myself. Even though she imprisoned me, perhaps I can still disrupt her plans and continue my own from down here. With a smile, I answered, "I believe I can help with your goblin trouble."

"Excellent," King Wendale said, taking a gulp of his beer. "With a dragon on our side, we're sure to eliminate those nasty buggers and reclaim our tunnels in no time." He held out his hand across the table to me. "Then we have a deal? I will have Arethil's remains sent to King Byron in exchange for your aid against our goblin infestation."

I shook his stubby hand to seal the deal, and my imprisonment within the Earth became just another step on my immortal journey.

ACT III

2011 AD

CHAPTER XVIII

REVELATION

We sat there across from Manius completely astonished by his story.

"Kieran's not," Manius said to me after clearly hearing my thoughts, "but then he saw everything from Dirk's memories." His attention turned to Kieran. "Didn't you?"

Kieran said nothing. I leaned forward to see him staring at the desk as if unsure what to do.

"Are you a god?" Kelena asked Vistilia bluntly.

Smiling at the question, she nodded towards me. "Why don't you ask Kevin? He has it figured out."

Kelena turned to me with a confused expression.

"I need to learn to keep my mind shut," I said with a laugh.

"What is she talking about? What is it you know?" Kelena asked me.

"Well," I began thinking back on Manius' story and what Vistilia had said to him millennia ago, "I think Vistilia is from another future of Earth."

Kelena's deepening look of confusion told me that I should explain further.

Taking a moment to think how to explain it, I told her, "All that we are and all that we know must be part of some kind of simulation from a future Earth where she lives."

"What?" Kelena asked, looking back at Vistilia.

She gave Kelena an agreeing nod. "Let me explain it differently. Within the next couple of decades, your scientists will create a computer program that simulates the life cycle of a universe. They will use this program to test many theories. The program will eventually be released to the public as an immersive virtual reality game where you can manipulate any and all aspects of it."

"So none of this is real?" Kelena asked, waving a hand at our surroundings.

"It's real to everything that resides here," Vistilia answered, "because this is all this universe's inhabitants know."

"You don't have the same godlike powers in your universe, do you?" I asked.

"No," she answered. "I am like any normal human here in this universe."

"How do you explain living for so long?" Kelena asked her.

"The scientists of my world have only recently tapped into the life extension technology to increase human life expectancy to 101 years of age. The reason I seem to have eternal life is because time flows differently within the simulation. What seems like a lifetime here is but a moment there."

"I bet you also look completely different in your world," I said to her.

"No. Actually, I look the same," she claimed cheerfully. "Most everyone can alter their genes to make minor changes to their appearance."

"Amazing," I whispered.

There was a brief silence before Manius leaned forward in his office chair, clasping his hands together on the desk. "I'll tell you what, Kieran," he began. "I'll make a deal with you."

We all remained quiet and listened for what Manius was about to propose.

"I will remove the bounty on Seraphine and all elves, if you give back Dirk."

"You can't be serious!" Kelena erupted.

Waving a hand to calm his sister, Kieran professed, "I can't bring him back the way I did Kelena."

"And why not?" Manius asked.

"I still had her body to reunite with her spirit," Kieran explained. "Dirk's body was destroyed when I absorbed him."

"Oh, Vistilia can give him a body," he stated.

"I can," she agreed while touching each of her fingernails to instantly paint flowers on them.

Kieran didn't answer right away, so Kelena expressed her disapproval. "After all those centuries, you finally gave that asshole what he deserved, and now you're considering allowing him back into this world?"

A single tear of blood tumbled down his cheek. "I've seen his memories and the motives behind his actions," Kieran explained. "He did what he believed was right."

"But that doesn't mean that he was right," Kelena argued.

"No, it doesn't, but I feel no better for killing him."

"If it helps you decide," Manius broke in, "I could have Vistilia strip all that was Dirk from you and continue hunting the elves that are passing as human."

Kelena sprang from her chair! "And I will tear the flesh from your bones!" she swore. Seeing Vistilia smile at the sudden excitement in the room, Kelena pointed at her. "And I don't care who you are, but I will char that pretty skin of yours!"

I remained quiet. I was growing afraid that this wouldn't turn out well.

With a calm voice, Vistilia said, "Kelena dear, don't be angry. You must have faith that everything will work out for the best."

"I have faith that we can manage on our own, thank you very much," she fired back, her eyes burning like hot coals.

Kieran took hold of her hand. "Kelena, please, this is what I must do."

She looked at her brother in complete shock. "You're not actually going to go through with this!"

Kieran didn't want to argue about it anymore. He had made his decision, and she wasn't going to change his mind.

She opened her mouth to say more but stopped herself. She stared at him for a moment before walking away to look out the window at the illuminated courtyard.

Kieran stood and placed a hand on my shoulder. "It will be all right, Kevin. Don't you worry," he said to me. He then nodded to Manius that he agreed to his terms.

Vistilia swiveled around in her office chair, and with a wave of her hand, the topographical globe began to slowly spin. A mist began to form around it that took on the appearance of clouds over the planet. I then realized that the globe was made of real water and dirt! She waved a finger that caused the world to spin faster, and she pointed to a spot where the elements pulled free of the globe and began to create a human form! Within moments, the globe was stripped to nothing, and a life-size clay sculpture of Dirk stood before us.

Manius and Vistilia stood from their chairs, so I got up and stood by the window with Kelena. Kieran stepped up to the clay sculpture of the man that tormented him for centuries. Without words, he stared into the lifeless eyes.

"All you have to do is pass through him," Vistilia instructed, "leaving behind all that is Dirk."

Kieran exhaled his apprehension, and his body became a transparent, ethereal fire before taking a step forward into the sculpture of Dirk. We watched as clay became flesh and what was lifeless became alive!

Kieran stepped out the other side, and his consistency returned to normal. The sculpture's eyes focused, and the mouth opened to take a deep breath! He collapsed to the floor, coughing and breathing heavily.

"Dirkonus," Manius spoke, "welcome back, son."

After taking a moment to catch his breath, Dirk

raised his head to look at us. His eyes fixed on Kieran. "You killed me," he said with bitter hatred.

"And I brought you back," Kieran responded gently.

"You should be grateful," Manius said to him.

"Shut up!" Dirk spat, standing before us. "You can see the future," he said, pointing an angry finger at Manius. "You sent him knowing he would kill me!"

"I sent him knowing he would bring you back," Manius defended his decision.

"That's how you got Eve killed!" Dirk yelled. "You put too much faith in the abilities that you got from that damned sorcerer! Well, your mistake was bringing me back . . . because I'm removing you from office."

Dirk raised an open hand at Manius but nothing happened. He strained to harm his dark father but was unable. "I'm weak. I need to feed," he assumed, examining his hand.

"No, Dirk," Kieran corrected him. "I kept your power."

"You shouldn't grow so dependent on magic," Manius repeated Dirk's warning. "It can only lead to ruin."

Shaking his head while looking at his powerless hands, Dirk refused to believe it. "No! NO!" Unsure of what to do, he ran!

"Let him go," Manius told us. "He'll be back." He then walked over to his desk and picked up the phone, pressing a single button on the base. "Yes, we have a minor problem this morning," he informed the person on the other end of the line. "There's a naked man running through the building. If he happens to find clothes before he's caught, he's about six feet with black hair. Please have him escorted off the premises. Thank you."

"Well, that was exciting," I said to break the tension still lingering in the room.

Vistilia nudged Manius with her elbow to get him to speak. "You have my word," he began suddenly, speaking to all of us. "I will immediately call for a meeting with my enforcers and order them to protect what few elves remain."

"How can we trust you after all you've done? What guarantee can you give us?" Kieran demanded.

"You'll just have to trust me," he answered plainly.

"I'll make sure he keeps his end of the bargain," Vistilia promised.

"And I don't trust you," Kelena said with a scornful laugh.

"How can I put your at ease?" Vistilia asked. "What can I do to earn your trust?"

"You can leave," Kelena answered coldly. "Speaking of which, I'm ready to leave," she said to her brother.

Kieran nodded that he too was ready and said to me, "Come on, Kevin. Let's get you home." He then turned to Manius. "If you go back on your word, and I learn that you or your thugs bring harm to an elf, I'll take you to the Sun myself. You may have gained my power to survive after the body is destroyed, but you won't like the transition," he warned before disappearing in a flash.

Kelena took my hand, but before she teleported me home, Vistilia said, "Don't you worry, Kevin.

Everything will be just fine."

A sudden bright light engulfed me, and we were gone.

CHAPTER XIX

PLAN OF ACTION

Kieran and Kelena were already sitting at the wrought iron table on my porch when my eyes adjusted from the brightness of teleporting. It was just before dawn, and I could hear buzzing mosquitoes in the air and the croaking tree frogs in the distance. Thankfully, mosquitoes are not attracted to vampires. I joined my friends at the table to discuss what we should do.

"From what Vistilia was telling us," Kieran began, "she didn't create the universe, but she has power over it."

"Like a kid playing a video game," I added.

"She abuses her power," Kelena said, fuming.

"Perhaps the scientists only observed, but it's just a game to her," Kieran explained.

Thinking of how crude our video games were compared to the simulation of an entire universe, I said,

"There's no telling how many other universes are out there."

"And how vastly different they could be," Kieran mentioned. "We should be thankful that this world isn't more hostile than what it is."

"I'm not thanking her for anything," Kelena spat. "If she wants to live in this universe, she should live as one of us. She shouldn't use her powers."

"According to Manius, she did just that," Kieran reminded her. "She lived one full human lifetime without using her powers. Afterwards, she made him a vampire, and I assume that she made other changes to the world, both before and after her life as a mortal."

"You know," I began, "her universe could just as well be a simulation of an even larger universe."

"Yeah, and she could just as well be lying about everything," Kelena commented.

"Kel, remember when you wanted to leave Sungrove?" Kieran asked. "You were tired of living the same life, day after day. You craved excitement. Vistilia no doubt comes to this world to escape her own. I mean, why would she want to live as a normal person in her world when she can live as a god here?"

"I suppose you're right," Kelena admitted. "But she sure allows a lot of death and suffering."

"Perhaps that's what drives the living," Kieran postulated. "That's what drove me. I accepted Sylvia's offer to become a vampire so that I may save you."

"What is it that drives you now?" I asked.

Kieran thought for a moment before answering, "Setting this world right."

"What seems right to us may not be to someone else," Kelena interjected.

"Few, if any, see the problems that we see, so they won't notice if we correct them," he quickly justified.

"What should we do now?" I asked.

Kieran answered, "Send an email to Seraphine. Tell her it's okay to see you. When she arrives, call for us."

"I can't wait to meet this elf," Kelena said, smiling at me.

"She's definitely a cool chick," I proclaimed.

"What's cool about her?" she questioned me.

"She's a geek like me," I answered with a big smile. "We can talk for hours about everything from advancements in technology to newly discovered habitable planets. We plan months in advance to see new science fiction and fantasy movies. We listen to the same bands. We even like playing the same video games! She's perfect, and she's hot!"

Both Kieran and Kelena laughed at my liveliness.

"There can't be many elves left in existence," Kieran mentioned. "Don't you find it peculiar that Vistilia matched you two up?"

A bit worried, I answered, "Yeah, now that you mention it."

"Why do you think Vistilia is showing interest in Kevin's love life?" Kelena asked.

"You mean lack of love life," I corrected her with a sad laugh. "She hasn't spoken to me in weeks! Knowing my luck with women, she probably has replaced me with a new man."

"QUIET!" she barked and then chuckled at her outburst. "Don't be so negative," she said to me, patting my hand.

"I hope she's okay," I said sadly.

"Don't give up hope," Kelena told me, standing to give me a hug.

The morning sun began to shine through to the patio furniture where we were sitting. I moved my leg to keep it out of the burning light.

"Well, I think it's about time to go inside," I told them. "You coming in?"

"No, I think we're going to attend Manius' meeting," Kieran answered, "and see if we can learn anything more about his omnipotent wife."

"And I think I'm going to challenge her to a good, old fashioned girl fight," Kelena joked, shaking her fist.

My eyes widened at her level of excitement. "I'd like to see that!"

"I'm sure you would," Kelena nodded with a teasing grin.

"Well, let's get going, Kel," her brother said, standing from his chair. "Kevin, we will see you soon."

"All right," I told them. "Be careful."

"We should be the ones telling you that," Kelena laughed.

"We won't be gone too long," Kieran said before he and his twin sister became transparent. They appeared as an ethereal fire, and instead of teleporting away, they took flight.

With the morning sun eating away at the darkness, I quickly ran to the door and stepped inside. I reached into my pocket and pulled out the folded pages where I took notes on Manius' story.

"I need to start writing this now while it's still

fresh on my mind, but first, I will email Seraphine," I said to myself and immediately went to my computer.

The mini fridge that Kelena brought me was next to my desk, and I remembered the many packs of blood in it. "I had almost forgotten about this," I said, opening the door to grab a pack. I went to the kitchen for a straw and inserted it into the pouch for a drink before returning to my desk.

EPILOGUE

It's been several days since Kieran and Kelena left to sit in at the meeting Manius was to have with his bounty hunters. Immediately after they left, I sent an email to Seraphine telling her that it was okay to see me, but she hasn't responded. I hope nothing bad has happened.

I've been spending most of my time writing Manius' epic tale. Even if he didn't give me permission, I would have still released it as my second book. It will make a great follow-up to Immortal Journey. I believe I will name it Immortal Conquest since Manius rid the world of Giants and overthrew Grimlash's tyrannical rule.

Suddenly feeling weak, I told myself, "I need to take a break." I opened my mini fridge but saw that I was out of blood. "Hmm, I guess I'll have to go hunting soon."

I rubbed my eyes and left my computer to go to the bathroom. I looked at myself in the mirror and saw that I looked dead. My eyes had turned milky white, and my skin had grayed.

"Oh, wow! I look terrible. How long have I been without blood?" I checked my watch to see what day it was. "I've lost track of time!" I said aloud to myself. "It's been over a week! I should go out right now for a drink."

I leaned over the sink and splashed my face with cold water. When I arose, I saw Dirk's reflection in the mirror standing behind me! I quickly turned around, but he raised a hand that held me in place by an invisible force! He wore a gauntlet that had a large, blue gem set in the palm.

"Good evening, Kevin," Dirk said calmly.

Through clenched teeth, I asked, "What do you want?"

"Don't be frightened. I'm not here to kill you, but I can't say this won't be painful."

Dirk closed the fingers of his gauntlet, and with a quick pull of his hand, he slammed me hard on the bathroom floor, cracking the tile beneath me. He stood over me and held the open palm of his enchanted gauntlet to my chest.

"Shhhh, this will all be over soon," he vowed. "I just need your power, so I can kill my father."

Suddenly, my blood boiled, and every muscle in my body cramped and twisted! Only a groan escaped my clenched teeth, but in my mind, I screamed in agony!

After what felt like an eternity of torture, the

pain finally ceased, and I opened my eyes to see Dirk still standing over me. He pulled a bone handled, red obsidian dagger from a leather sheath on his belt. He held the dagger with both hands and stared at it for a moment. He then turned the dagger toward himself and plunged it into his heart! He gasped and fell across me before slowly crumbling to dust. A strange fire rose from the ashes and took shape above me. Dirk had the phoenix fire that Kieran had passed to me!

"I had a feeling you would one day serve a purpose," he said with a smile.

In a blinding flash, he teleported away.

My entire body hurt. I could barely move, much less get up. I remained on the floor an hour or more before I heard someone knock on the door.

"Help!" I cried out. "Help me!"

The door was kicked in, and someone ran through the house to the bathroom where I still lay, covered in Dirk's ashes.

"Oh no!" I heard Seraphine exclaim when she saw me. She rushed to my side and lifted my head from the floor.

"You came back," I said faintly.

"Because I love you," she answered, caressing my face.

I broke into tears as she kissed my lips and then my nose.

"Kevin!" she said with a look of shock. She wiped the tears from my face and held her hand out for me to see the clear liquid on her fingers. "You're mortal."

THE IMMORTAL EPIC

WILL CONTINUE WITH

IMMORTAL GENESIS